This book is dedicated to the tragedians of the city.

And the party at the end of the world.

Setlist
The Stone Dandelions
London, UK, 2nd July 2023

Chapter One. Cold Dark Earth

Richard was late to the funeral. Seeing his coal-black suit and kohl-rimmed eyes one might be inclined to say fashionably late, but it was uncharacteristic for Richard to be pulling up in a Hansom carriage to a vista of smoked-stained columns, narrow-arched windows and churning grey clouds half an hour into the proceedings. Richard had not been to many funerals, not because had not known many people who had died, but because he tended not to be invited. He wasn't entirely certain how people were supposed to be invited to funerals. Were there paper invitations? Maybe you had to be in the

Richard tried to stand still. This was no time for fidgeting. If there was ever a time for cool professionalism it was now. Layne was eccentric, and they definitely liked him but if he did not handle this well his job was on the line. He took a deep breath. 'And you didn't want any photos or to say anything specific?'

Layne frowned contemplatively. They flicked a glance in the direction of the dead man's brother. 'You can make something up if you feel like you need to.'

Richard looked back at the open grave and the beveled steel-grey casket, softly shadowed in the smoothly overcast light. He imagined what his embellished press release might look like.

SCENE of Death—American rock band The Stone Dandelions discover mysterious dead body of man who died during London concert. Lead singer Layne calls unknown man's death 'very mysterious and tragic and enigmatic and dolorous' Layne 'sends love to his family unless his family are awful people in which case Layne does not send love and instead sends bad vibes but wants everybody to have a nice evening'

'Really?'

Layne's brow furrowed. 'No, probably not.'

What would the papers want to hear? Richard had started out as a journalist for a local paper in a small town in the Midlands where any event could be sensationalized to make it seem like something important or exciting or even dangerous was going on, but this was London. You didn't court controversy in London. It would either pass you by or come knocking on your door on its own terms. He also wasn't a journalist anymore. Layne could do whatever they wanted even if he didn't understand it.

'I'm going to talk to his brother,' he decided.

'His name is Alan Douglas,' Layne told him.

The young man startled at being approached.

'Hey Alan,' Richard said softly, 'I'm Richard, I'm part of Layne's team.'

'Do you know if— If the rest of the band are going to show up?' Alan asked.

Now this was a different angle. If the man who was found in the parking lot was a fan, Richard was looking at an entirely different story. 'Mila and Kiran are happy to come to the funeral reception if you would want them to be there.'

Alan swallowed. 'So, this was just Layne Thompson's idea?'

'Are you a fan?' Richard asked, unsure if this was the right question to be asking.

Alan shrugged. 'I've heard some of their stuff on Radio 2. Thought it was pretty good. Robert wasn't really into music.'

'What did he do?'

Alan shook his head. 'He moved to London a month ago because he met a girl. He was working at a bar. Then she ghosted him, apparently.'

This was interesting. Potentially significant. 'What was her name?' Richard asked.

'He didn't tell me.'

'So you weren't that close, then?' Richard was internally kicking himself even as he asked the question.

'He was a loner. He wasn't a very well-adjusted bloke. Not a lot of friends.'

'That must be hard.' Richard said.

Alan rubbed his eyes with the back of his hands. 'Like you said, we weren't that close.'

'Still hard. Did he go to church?' Richard was still worrying about the service. It felt so denominational for a funeral when so little was known about the person it was for.

Alan closed his eyes made a vague gesture in the direction of his brother's casket. 'Not really, but he was basically Christian.'

Richard nodded 'In that case, may he rest in peace.'

Alan gave him a strange look.

'What is it?'

'You're just so awkward. I feel like I'm being interviewed,' Alan sighed.

'You're not. But—' Richard hesitated. 'If you were, is there anything that I should know about Robert?' he asked. It wasn't as though he could make things any more awkward.

Alan looked up at the solid grey sky, impassively at first and then a wave of emotion seemed to come over him and he was blinking back tears. 'He tried to be better. Robert tried to be better.'

Layne handed Kiran the tissue.

Kiran stared at it, trying to decipher the constellation of symbols Layne had constructed between the lines of text. 'I can't read your handwriting,' she observed.

'Hmm,' Layne said disbelievingly.

'Are you sure you can even read your own handwriting?' Kiran asked. 'Is that why you're always writing on your phone or your computer?'

Layne was crestfallen. 'This one isn't even that messy.'

'And what are these markings?' Kiran pointed at the symbols between the lines of text.

'Those are my thoughts— Indicating my thoughts for what might be happening with the melody and instrumentation.'

'They're not words,' Kiran realised. The markings were mostly lines and circles and squiggles of varying amplitudes.

Kiran held the tissue further from her face and squinted at it. Layne reached for the tissue. 'No, not words' they agreed, 'they're representations of what I'm thinking.'

Understanding dawned as Kiran stopped trying to interpret the symbols as standing for anything she could identify. 'Did you invent a new mode of musical notation?' she asked.

Layne wasn't sure if Kiran was impressed or amused. She was smiling. They took that as a good sign. 'I— Well, yes, I invented it, but it's not new, I've been using it for years.'

'How have I never seen you do this before now?' she was definitely impressed now.

Layne blushed and waved a hand dismissively. 'Because I'm better at verbally explaining my ideas.'

Kiran set the tissue back down on the table. 'Are you embarrassed?'

'Absolutely not. I've just been informed that I've invented a new mode of musical notation!' Layne's voice squeaked at the end of the sentence. Then Layne put a hand over their face and gazed intently down at the table.

This was impossibly endearing. Kiran took a sip from her drink, wondering what she could write based on what Layne had drawn on the tissue if they gave her no other explanation. 'How were you thinking of these markings before?'

Layne shrugged. 'I guess I was just thinking of it as some scribbles on a piece of paper? Just kind of drawing the sound.'

'That's so cool though. That way you can just get down what you're thinking right when it occurs to you.' Kiran took out her own notebook and opened it on the table beside the ink-drenched tissue. 'Do you think we can do this with two guitars?'

Mila took a bite of her burrito, stared philosophically into space for several seconds, and then poured more salsa into it.

Weeks later, Mila was grateful she had kept her receipt, and that the Chipotle employees remembered her signature to verify the payment from her AmEx card in Kiran's green glitter gel pen.

Chapter Three. The Lovers Reversed

Walking through London at night, Richard felt held, as though the city itself were applying pressure to all the open wounds on his psyche. He felt like he was being wrapped in bandages, bound, and suspended until there was no room left to be afraid. No room to chafe and jostle. Like he was a correctly installed gear. Like he was some small organ of the breathing multitude. Or something caught in a spiderweb of steel cable. He just had to catch his breath and the bus that would take him home.

The air was warm on his skin, heavy and sour with fertilizer and the scent of butterfly bush. The shrivelled skeletons of dead leaves from past autumns drifted out of gardens on a breeze and skimmed the sidewalks. A sheet of cardboard that had escaped from a recycling pile crossed the street like a sail, followed by a ponderous pigeon. All the complications and confusions of his own life existed on the same plane as foxes with bottlebrush fur digging pizza crusts out of bins. He felt like that sometimes, like he had just followed his nose to something that smelled appealing. There was a kind of harmony in that. A feeling that he had become a kind of city animal by adaptation. He hoped that was true, that he really had adapted to his surroundings, that he was living as he was meant to and that he could make the people around him happy.

It was even warmer on the bus than it was outside. All of the seats downstairs were full, so he climbed the steps holding on to both railings as the bus began to move. Compared to the buses in the towns Richard had grown up in, riding the red double-deckers felt like standing on a cloud drifting smoothly across the pavement, but he was not very coordinated, so he held on tightly anyway.

Most of the seats were full in the top of the bus as well so he sat beside someone who fell asleep in the next few minutes with an open beer can in their hand and snored for most of the rest of the journey. He wondered how they would know when to get off the bus, but maybe they rode this bus every day and had an instinct for where they were regardless of whether or not they were actually conscious. Or perhaps—and this was the more likely scenario—they were simply too drunk to care where they ended up. Stains on the fabric of the seats on the bus were of no concern to Richard. It was not as though the stains, whatever had caused them, could actually hurt him, none of them appeared to be recent, although he wondered sometimes if the seats were ever cleaned or replaced.

Richard never wanted to be the person to request a stop on the bus, so he would almost always wait to stand up until someone else had pressed the red button and the 'bus stopping' notice had appeared on the screen. This had, on a few occasions, resulted in Richard getting off the bus several streets away from where he was trying to go. He didn't mind this too much as long as he did not end up getting lost. Tonight, there were other people getting off at his stop, a benefit of living near a train station.

There was still water pooled at the edges of the road from the rain and he leapt over the puddles, a move that, if it made him look ridiculous, at least made him look ridiculous in an exciting way. Or so he hoped. It turned a few heads, someone in a black suit leaping about like a child playing hopscotch or skipping rope. They generally looked away once they saw Richard walking purposefully at a more ordinary pace. It was almost like they thought their eyes might have been playing tricks on them. That was one thing he loved about being in the city. No one really cared about how strange he was, and once people figured out what they were looking at—for instance someone with worn out shoes trying to avoid putting his foot in a puddle—the novelty wore off and they did not consider it worth commenting on. It was a great relief to be one local weirdo among many and to be considered just another patch of the fabric of the place rather than singled out as the gloomy, studious figure who walked around in the rain and spent all day in the library not speaking to a soul. That was the thing about big cities, Richard considered, you think someone is weird until you move to the city and then they're just another person. They're strange because that's just what people are like and there is no pressure for them to explain themselves.

Of course, not everyone agreed with this point of view. The things people shouted at each other could be comparatively extreme. When Richard really did not care what anyone thought of him he would dance down the street and sometimes he would have to stop to write down the elaborate threats he heard muttered in his direction.

When Richard arrived home, Shamira Allis was lying on the sofa. While this was something Shamira did often, but it generally did not happen until much later at night. Typically, when Richard came home his partner had a laptop open and was working or she had turned on the TV and was watching with such single-minded intensity that she would not even hear Richard come in. Shamira wasn't asleep. She was staring blankly at the wall, eyes unfocused. She would have been lying full-length but the couch was too short.

'Shamira. What's up?'

Shamira stirred, eyes still boring into the wall, but now she was actually seeing it. 'There's a lawsuit against me.'

'What?' Richard said automatically.

'A lawsuit,' Shamira repeated.

'Yeah, I heard, that's why I said "what?"'

'For plagiarism.' Shamira clarified.

'What did you plagiarize?' In Richard's opinion, Shamira's work was so far from being derivative that it seemed to have nothing to do with anything else anyone had ever written or possibly even thought about.

'I didn't plagiarize anything, but I've got a show that's just opened on the West End.'

Richard frowned. Shamira's play had been well-received, if by 'well received' you meant receiving a healthy assortment of five star reviews on microblogging platforms and one, two and three star reviews in national papers. 'Someone thinks you stole *These Flowers Might Be Ours*?'

Shamira squirmed into a more upright position. 'They've got a dated manuscript of someone else's play from 2018.'

'No way.' Richard was baffled, feeling as though his mind was failing to compute. If his thoughts were a mouse on an old

ghosts. He *almost* felt like something might be happening that did not have a so-called rational or scientific explanation.

Shamira conversed with the ghosts she knew were haunting their flat. There was an old man who had passed away shortly before the flat was renovated, a little girl who had died of cholera in the nineteenth century, and several people who had worked the land in centuries past when this part of London was agricultural fields.

A crash came from the bedroom and Richard startled as though he had been electrically shocked. 'What was that?'

Shamira made a face. 'I stacked some boxes improperly.'

Richard's lips twitched into a smirk. 'Put a larger one on top of a smaller one?'

Shamira made an appeal in defense of her reason. 'I ordered some more pots and pans. They just arrived.'

'And so, what, you just decided to put the larger box on top of the pile of smaller boxes of things you ordered?' Richard's teasing was full of a sort of affectionate awe that anyone could do anything so absurd.

'Well, I opened most of them,' Shamira pointed out.

Richard grinned. 'Did you unpack most of them too and just leave the boxes lying around?'

'Well, it's not like we've got a huge amount of storage.' This was true, there wasn't so much as a broom cupboard anywhere in their flat.

Richard hummed in agreement. A teetering pile of cardboard boxes hardly qualified as storage.

Shamira chimed in with a hypothetical 'I'm not saying this is a storage system either, but if it weren't there, I'm sure I would find some other way of creating organizational chaos.'

'D'you think?' Richard considered this assertion gravely.

'I'd go back to leaving my clothes in a pile on the floor,' Shamira speculated.

'I can't believe you actually did that.'

'It was a disaster. I'd trip over piles of clothes! Multiple times a day!'

'I concede! I give in!'

Shamira laughed as there was another crash as the box in the other room finished toppling over. 'I'm going to go check if anything is broken.'

There was a knocking on the door outside. This startled Richard, causing him to jump and then unnerved him by not stopping after the typical three or four knocks. He spun around and ran down the stairs two at a time. Opening the door, he looked out into the empty night. There was nothing on the doorstep. He looked up and down the street. Aside from parked cars, it was empty in both directions.

Richard's heart pounded in his chest, from agitation rather than from sprinting down the stairs. He tried to slow down his breathing. This was clearly some form of ding-dong ditching someone had decided to play on people whose doorbells didn't work. Slowly, he closed the door and inhaled deeply, letting out a long breath.

Shamira stood at the top of the stairs and looked down at him, tilting her head to one side. 'Are you good? You alright?'

Richard looked up, biting his lip. 'Did you hear knocking?'

Shamira shook her head.

Richard sighed. 'That's fun.'

'You heard knocking?'

'I heard a lot of knocking, like someone was trying bang the door down.'

'Do you think you could have heard something else and interpreted it as knocking?'

Richard's gaze was full of something baleful and long-suffering that Shamira didn't want to think of as 'haunted.' He shook his head. 'Honestly, Shamira, I have no idea.'

'I'm sorry,' Shamira said.

Richard sniffed. 'You're sorry that I'm hearing things?'

'I am!'

'Well, that's something at least,' Richard said, trying not to sound bitter.

'Someone could have been out there, or—' Shamira thought about what she was going to say and decided against it.

'Or I can see things that other people can't see?'

Shamira paused, waiting for Richard to hear what he had just said, and then, hesitantly suggested, 'Er, wouldn't that be hear things other people can't hear?'

'Whatever.'

'You know I didn't say that,' she said slowly.

'I know you didn't, but you thought about it.'

'I don't want you to be afraid.' Shamira said as though this was not an ominous thing to say.

'I know.'

'If it's worth anything, I don't think your grip on reality is slipping.'

'How would you know?' Richard asked, letting some bitterness slip through the floodgates, 'You know I'm really good at hiding what I'm going through."

'You say that all the time, but I don't think it's true. I know when you're hurting. I can see it and it hurts to see that you're afraid and that you don't trust yourself.' Shamira took a couple of steps down the stairs towards Richard. He gripped the stairwell railing, unsure of how to take this all it.

'You think I'm hearing ghosts,' Richard said, more derisively than he intended to.

'I didn't say that,' Shamira repeated.

'But you think it.'

Shamira let out a small sigh of surrender. 'Look, I don't know what you want me to say.'

'I get it. You think this house is haunted. That's fine. I don't really know what to do with that information.'

'Well, you could write down the things you notice. You might discover some a pattern that could give you some sort of insight—'

'But what if I'm really just hallucinating? You know I've had hallucinations before. If I try to find patterns in things that don't exist while my mind is already trying to generate patterns that don't exist, it's not going to help anything, is it? It's just going to make it harder for me to tell what is real and what isn't.'

'But you've always been such a good judge of what's happening. You don't misinterpret things.'

Richard put his head in his hands. 'Shamira, no one should go around believing that they can't misinterpret what's happening around them.'

'But that's no reason to start out by assuming what you're experiencing isn't real either.'

Richard looked up, tears pricking in the corners of his eyes. 'Isn't it?'

Shamira felt as though Richard had just pulled the anchor of the conversation out of the sea and was letting it bang against the side of the boat. She sat down heavily on the carpeted steps. 'You sounded so rational until just now.'

Richard snapped his fingers sarcastically. 'Did I? Damn it. I thought I was doing so well.'

Shamira was not about to let him turn this into a joke. She shook her head. 'You *were* doing so well.'

Carefully, Richard sat down on the step just below the one Shamira was sitting on. 'And now I'm slipping again, is that it?'

Shamira moved her hand to Richard's shoulder. 'Richard, you're really smart, you just sometimes have an over-active imagination.'

'I have an over-active imagination?' Richard leaned into Shamira's hand. He was on the verge of bitter laughter. 'Shamira, some days I feel like I can hardly imagine anything.'

She just wanted Richard to feel alright. A frown creased the skin between her brows. She had no solutions to offer, so she was left with saying what she believed. 'That's not true,' she said.

Richard looked away from her. 'I said that was how I feel, you can't tell me that isn't how I feel. Sometimes I feel barren, bereft of inspiration, empty, like a husk that the seeds have already been torn out of but is still clinging to the plant in some futile effort not to slip out of existence and crumble into nothing.'

'I don't see you that way at all. You have a very strong sense of self.'

Richard had been told this many times, but he still reacted as though he had never considered that anyone could possibly see him that way. In the dimly lit stairwell, he felt almost as though he could sink through the floor and disappear if he wished hard enough. 'Really?' he breathed. Slowly, he got back up on his feet. He held the railing, steadying himself. 'I feel like I am scarcely able to scrape together the semblance that I know how to proceed in day-to-day life.'

'Well, you know you're not alone in that. I expect most people feel that way to a greater or lesser extent.'

Richard brushed Shamira away. 'I don't know where you get all these platitudes minimalizing or dismissing how I'm trying to tell you I feel. You don't get to tell me that everyone feels that way when I tell you I'm in torment.'

'Hey!' Shamira shouted and then caught herself. 'I might not be expressing myself very clearly but I— That's not what I meant—'

'If you say something about imposter syndrome, I swear I am going to walk out that door right now.'

'I wasn't going to. I was going to say maybe we should go upstairs and put on a movie or something.'

'Distract ourselves?' There was something in Richard's gaze that Shamira could not place. A kind of fire that could warm or burn depending on how careful you were.

'We could put on a film to watch because I would like to watch a film this evening. You can decide whether or not this is something you want to do.' Shamira closed her eyes and realised after closing them how much tension and pressure had built up behind her eyelids.   'Please don't yell at me.'

'I'm not going to yell at you. What do you want to watch?' Richard's voice was full of concession—full of gentleness.

Shamira did not open her eyes right away. She remained sitting on the staircase, leaning against the wall. Stillness was a relief. When she did move to stand up the floorboards creaked and seemed to write a concluding sentence to the argument—if it could be called an argument—they had just had.

Richard was waiting upstairs. 'I would like to be able to cry. What movie do you think would make me cry tonight?' When he was in the right mood Richard was often taken by surprise by how easily he cried, feeling like a wellspring that had been building up for eons had finally found an outlet.

'You're lovely, you know that?' Shamira said, sitting down beside him and picking up the blanket that had fallen on the floor.

'If you say so,' Richard said, not feeling like there was any evidence of this, but considering believing it because Shamira said so. Maybe he was like the ghosts in the walls—Shamira would believe in him even when no one else did.

Chapter Four. Page Turner

On the night of Saturday, the second of July, the Oxford Circus carpark was nearly full. Five of the crew members running The Stone Dandelions show had parked their cars there in the morning and not returned until after the show. The rest of the carpark was filled with people who were in Central London for all sorts of reasons.

The very brief attempt by the metropolitan police to determine who was in the carpark when the body was discovered found three people interviewing for the same job at a national bank, a stockbroker getting a grand piano restrung, an elderly woman taking her dog to get her favorite ice cream, a family of eight going to see *The Book of Mormon*, an antiquarian who claimed to be having a 'rare book emergency' and an undergraduate who had filled the boot of his car with whisky and vodka, supposedly 'for a large house party'.

When Richard arrived, there were police barricades up around the stagehand Geoff's car. As he got closer, he could see, at the center of the swarm of activity, the body of a man lying against the back wheels of Geoff's car. Richard's first thought was that the man had been stuck by the vehicle, possibly run over, but the more he looked, the more the geometry of the scene did not make sense.

The man collapsed on the pavement—and from the apparent stiffness of the body, dead for hours—was too close to the vehicle to have been thrown away from it by an impact. There was no blood or sign of any external injury. He appeared to have simply collapsed while walking behind the vehicle. Possibly from sudden heart failure.

It seemed odd to Richard that the body could have lain out in the open for hours in such a busy area, but then again, it was Central London, and, furthermore it was Soho, and no one wanted to ruin their night by getting involved with someone else's problems. But surely at least one person would have called 999 earlier? Richard wondered if he was still thinking like he was in his village of five hundred people. Could it be that in London no one would take care of you unless you got lucky? Was that just the way it was? That people keeping to themselves was blessing and a curse?

Geoff was being half-heartedly questioned by the police. Somewhat pointlessly, Richard asked 'Is he dead?'

'Dead for five or six hours apparently,' Geoff told him.

Richard stared at the body, unable to look away. The man's face was slack and waxy. Richard could not imagine what it would have looked like when he was alive. The man was young, not much older than Richard, and he was athletic—goes-to-the-gym-and-has-a-personal-trainer-athletic, not works-a-physical-job athletic—he wore a grey t-shirt, possibly an undershirt, and dark orange trousers. There did not appear to be anything in his pockets.

Layne had clearly seen the police cars because they ran into the parking lot, and then stood, a little unsteadily, as though their ankles might give out from running in platform boots.

'Someone died here?' they said, swaying from side to side.

Richard had seen dead people before, but usually it was in a hospital, and usually they had not been dead for as long as the man lying on the pavement. He wondered if he was actually smelling the putrefaction of hours under the sun or if he was just imagining it.

'Do we know who he was?' Layne asked. They seemed to be seeing something Richard could not. Maybe they could imagine what the man would have been like when he was alive.

'Are you alright?' Geoff asked them.

The police did not seem to recognize Layne, which Richard was relieved by. They asked Layne to step away, which they did, assuring Geoff that they were fine. They then seemed to realise that Richard was standing there too and asked him to leave as well. He followed Layne up the street.

Layne walked quickly, as though frightened of being noticed, which they were, but they typically managed to disguise it by walking as though they had somewhere very important to be, which, according to themself, they often did.

Richard did not dare talk to them when they was acting like this, so he followed them at what he hoped was a comfortable, companionable distance. It became clear after a few twists and turns that Layne was mostly walking to calm and comfort themself. At one point they stopped outside of a shuttered café and very slowly, deliberately looked at him as if to say, 'you can keep following me if you want, but you're not going to get very much out of it.'

Richard was not sure what to do after that and ended up at the hotel bar. He saw Layne go up to her room and then he stepped back out into the street to take the night bus home. Shamira was asleep when he got there.

The morning after Shamira received the take-down letter from the theatre in Boston, Violet stared into the mirror and tucked her hair behind her ears.

Yesterday she went by Richard. Today she was Violet. She had first heard of genderfluidity when she was in high school and social media was still a wild frontier. Reading about the idea of someone's gender identity shifting over time, she had realised that was what she experienced. Some days masculinity, a distinctly queer masculinity that reminded Violet of the smooth surface of stainless steel, crushed pine needles and the smell of gasoline, led Richard out into the open. He was a gentle man, straightforward and happily a little bit boring. When she went by Violet she was also gentle, straightforward and something of a bore, but she leaned a bit more into the unconventional on those days. Violet, who swore exceptionally rarely, was fond of the term 'genderfuck.' She was a woman who was a man the day before and for all she knew would be a man again by the next morning. The more she had been able to express herself, the more certain she was that she was doing what was right for herself. She found new moments of euphoria every day.

She had felt like she was pretending to be someone else for so long—that every day she was putting on a performance. She had wondered sometimes if this feeling of performing, of hiding who she really was most of the time, meant that she would be a good actor. Then there had come a day when she felt like she had been introduced to the entirety of herself. She could never fit into just one narrative, just one way of expressing herself. Then a day came that she realised she did not need to, that she would never have to pick a side and could follow what made her comfortable, knowing in her heart who she really was. In her memory that day was gilded and illuminated. It was as though a mask had been lifted from her face and a disguising cloak had been plucked from her body. Violet had felt like everyone could see right through her on that day, through to the core of herself. As though a naked soul had walked the street, undefined by flesh or thought.

As far as Violet could tell, there wasn't much of a pattern to whether she was one gender or another and shifts in how she was feeling about her gender occurred days or months apart. She looked in the small round mirror balanced in front of the frosted glass of the bathroom window and smirked at her reflection. She adjusted the black rubber choker around her neck and considered putting on lipstick.

Violet had worried a great deal when she was younger about whether she, as a genderfluid person who sometimes identified with her assigned gender at birth, was 'trans enough' or 'queer enough' to acknowledge those aspects of her identity. It had kept her awake at night for months. But as she had grown older, she had realised that there were not any rules governing queer identities and there weren't any boxes you had to try to fit into and that was the entire point. Realizing she had free rein to express herself however she wanted had given her confidence she never would have known she could possess. Looking now at her face in the mirror, a smug, sardonic, comfortable expression glinting back at her, she could hardly remember the terrified young person she had seen in the glass only a few years earlier. She could hardly have imagined that she could have ended up feeling this comfortable in her own skin. She remembered shaking so badly she could hardly stand and turning the lights off so she could bear to be in a room with a mirror or take a shower. It was a dangerous thing to do, shower in the dark, because Violet had always been quite clumsy. There had been a day when she had slipped and hit her head, but she had not told anyone about that. There hadn't been any blood and she had barely lost consciousness.

These days she dressed however made her feel incredible. She was resolved to be the person she would have needed to see when she was younger.

She was still terrified for her safety and career prospects. As confident and comfortable as she now felt, she knew that most people did not understand.

'I've been reading more about this,' Violet said, pouring a glass of orange juice, realizing she had just brushed her teeth and staring at it regretfully. 'It seems like most of the time people go to court to clear their name.'

'The lawyer says we should capitulate to the take-down request if we don't want to get dragged through court for years,' Shamira said.

'Did you tell him the show was on the West End?' Violet demanded.

'The lawyer's a woman and she is aware. The show's probably closing in a couple months anyway.' Shamira told her.

'But this could spell the end of your career. You made it this far. You can't give up now!' Violet was nearly shouting.

'I can do whatever I want.'

'Well, yes, obviously, but you should at least try. This was your dream. This was an actual dream come true.'

'They have a pretty strong case. The lawyer really thinks I should drop it and I think she's right. Otherwise, I won't just have a production close, I will be deep in debt and no one will trust anything I bring forward," Shamira argued.

Violet looked wounded. 'But you're not the only one you have to think about. What about everyone else working on the show? It's become a big commercial production. That's nearly a hundred people.'

'It's not exactly selling out, is it? It's too niche. Experimental absurdist queer theatre about quantum mechanics and a gardener in the eighteenth century was never going to be a box office hit. It probably should never have had a transfer. From a financial standpoint it was a very poor business decision.'

'Someone took a risk on you! Someone really cared.'

Shamira shrugged, resigned to defeat. 'No one really cared, they thought it was going to be a star vehicle. They thought they could get some big celebrity from the television who wanted to be seen as quirky and interesting and relevant.'

'Maybe, but it went ahead even though they didn't get anyone famous.' Violet opened the refrigerator door to put the orange juice away.

'I'm almost certain someone dropped out at the last minute, and they decided I didn't need to know.'

'Someone dropped out—Who do you think it was? Who would you want it to have been?'

'I don't care about any of that, I just want someone who connects to the script. If they brought in a big audience that would be terrifying—I mean exciting, but I just want someone who could give an authentic performance.'

'You're going to convince—or I guess your lawyer or whoever is going to convince a West End production to close just because of some letter? While it's making them money?'

Shamira sharply closed the refrigerator door. 'It's not making them money.'

'What?' Violet gasped.

'It's been a commercial loss. A box office flop.'

'Don't say that.'

'Why not? It's true.'

'You shouldn't speak negatively about your own work.'

Shamira rolled her eyes. 'The production is losing money. I don't mind. It's no skin off my nose. Or it wasn't until now. I've gotten paid. The production was probably going to close early anyway.'

'But the critics adored it.' Violet was flailing. The past couple months had seemed too good to be true and now it seemed like all of Shamira's fears were coming true.

'Some of them, maybe, but that doesn't make the theatre any money.'

Violet scraped the bottom of the barrel of optimism. 'Things could pick up again in a couple of weeks.'

'Violet. Don't you understand? I'm actually devastated and you're just making it worse.'

Violet raised both eyebrows, an expression of profound shock and dismay. 'I'm so sorry!'

'I'm just trying to make it through this with what is left of my dignity and reputation because unlike you, people don't just assume that I'm competent and capable.'

'Well. I'm not going to let you.'

Shamira blinked. 'Excuse me?'

'I'm not going to let you get away. You're going to stand up for yourself and fight this out until the bitter end.'

'I thought I explained why that was a terrible idea.'

'You wrote the play. No one gets to take that away from you."

'Violet, you're being unreasonable.'

'No. I'm not.'

Shamira sighed. 'This isn't about you. This is my decision to make.'

'I'm not about to let you just slink away because someone's challenged you on something.'

'It's not a challenge, it's a lawsuit.'

Violet pulled the refrigerator door open again, half as a dramatic flourish, half looking for more breakfast. 'A lawsuit that you could win!'

'My lawyer doesn't think so.'

'I know you wrote the play. Everyone knows you wrote the play.'

Shamira slammed the refrigerator door shut. 'I don't understand why you feel like you can tell me what to do.'

'I'm not telling you what to do.'

'You quite literally are—'

'I'm telling you what I'm not going to let you do.'

Shamira scoffed, a sound of scandalised disbelief 'I don't need your permission to do anything. You're not my mother. This is absurd.'

Violet smiled a slow, smug smile. 'Oh, I don't think you understand. I'm not denying you permission to do anything. I'm threatening to be disappointed in you.'

'Oh.' A sharp inhalation from Shamira. 'Oh, I see.'

'I'm not going to do anything. You know that. I will simply... feel disappointment.'

'I'm going to ask when she thinks the court dates would be.'

'There you go.'

'There's something wrong with you, Violet.' Shamira said, dialing the lawyer's number.

'Believe me, I'm aware.' Violet nodded agreeably.

'It's kind of terrifying.'

'I don't mean to be terrifying.'

'Are you sure about that?'

The lawyer answered the phone. 'I think I understand everything you've told me— No, you don't need to go over it again. I would like to move forward with the case. Yes, I'm sure. Well, I understand that you'd like me to think about it longer, but I have made my decision—' Shamira ended the call. 'I really wonder what I have gotten myself into this time.'

'This is exciting!' Violet clapped.

'We're going to end up tens of thousands of pounds in debt. That isn't exciting.'

Violet shook her head. 'We're going to win a lawsuit and then people will think twice about ever coming after you.'

'It's not the responsible thing to be doing.'

'It's the courageous thing to be doing.'

'Yeah, according to you. You're not the one who's, uh, everything would be on the line.'

Violet reached for the handle on the refrigerator door again. 'Layne could bail us out.'

'Layne Thompson? Violet, Layne's crazy.'

Violet looked at her partner skeptically. 'That's a pretty ableist argument to make.'

'I didn't mean it that way.'

'Yeah you did, but so what? Layne's got the money. We wouldn't have to worry. What have we got to lose?'

'My credibility, for one thing.'

Violet let go of the fridge door handle. 'You wouldn't be losing your credibility; you would be defending it.'

Chapter Five. Yeah, You Should Probably Get That Looked At

Autumn wished she had invested in more comfortable furniture. The sofa her clients sat on was nice, if worn out and 'pre-loved' before Autumn had ever laid eyes on it, but her own chair was not suited to a conversation as long as this one. Layne had been telling her about the body that had been discovered after the show at the Palladium.

The practice Autumn worked with had been renting theses double-zoned rooms in Islington for three years now. It was very private, almost informal and the rooms looked like someone's grandmother's sitting room, which was probably what they had been before they were occupied by a half dozen therapists. Sometimes Autumn thought she should buy a tin of biscuits and fill it with sewing scissors and pincushions just to complete the effect.

But Autumn did not have sewing scissors and pincushions. Instead, she had a degree in psychology, so she sat on the hard wooden chair and listened intently to the musician sprawled on the threadbare couch. Layne had been in to see Autumn every week since the beginning of The Stone Dandelions' UK tour.

'His brother ended up getting in touch with me online. Because Robert was found by our crew. He said he wanted to make sure that I was okay, which I was really moved by. I wanted to be like, no, I'm the one who should be checking in on you—you just lost your brother. I don't think I realised how rattled I was until after he had said that to me. I almost felt like he had given me permission to be affected by what had happened. I was really grateful to him. I asked if there was anything I could do, if I could pay for the funeral—'

Autumn sat forward in her chair. 'Do you think it was a drug overdose?'

Layne was taken aback. 'I'm sorry, what?'

'What do you think was the cause of death?' Autumn pursued.

Layne closed their eyes and inhaled deeply through their nose. 'Autumn, this isn't a murder investigation.'

Autumn raised an eyebrow. 'It isn't?'

loom so large in their imaginations that they scrutinize every move looking for a fault they can dig their fingers into. That's scary. I think it would be scary for anyone. I haven't really had stalkers, or anyone threaten violence— I know a lot of people who have, I know I know I've been very lucky.'

'People who search the names of people they're obsessed with, people they have a para-social relationship—half the time they're looking to feel betrayed by the person they're so obsessed with but if they find someone finding fault with something that they don't agree is a fault they are so quick to pounce and it really doesn't help or serve anything,' Autumn observed.

Layne nodded and continued their diatribe. 'When people are actually awful—and we have different opinions of what constitutes actually being awful, a lot of people in the mainstream adulation I consider to be actually awful people even though I have never met them which might arguably not be fair, but I know that their actions have consequences, even if they don't. That's what it's about for me understanding the balance between consequences and intent. Some people mean to do harm, some people knowingly perpetuate a great deal of harm. Other people are willfully ignorant, and some people have caused so much damage unintentionally that that they really should not be in a position where it is possible for them to cause that much harm again. That's really what it comes down to for me. Some people get put on pedestals, but I think often that pedestal is just labelled 'decent reasonable person' which is why it hurts so much when it crumbles because it's not just a mistake, it's often something terrible, something that has genuinely caused a massive amount of harm. Because we can't assume that anyone is not a terrible person. That seems to be how it is. Which is a disheartening thought, but you can't dwell on it. That won't get you anywhere. The world is much stranger, I think, than a lot of people give it credit for.

'So, I don't want anyone to feel betrayed. I've thought a lot about what I could do to avoid making anyone feel betrayed, like I had broken any kind of promise to our audience and I figured that almost anything I did would actually end up leaving some people feeling betrayed because people have built such a pedestal—I hate using that word and I don't even know that if it's accurate because it's definitely not a vision of infallibility, it's more like this idea that I'm to be held to the most exacting, or frankly puritanical standards because I am in the public eye and the media tries to drum up controversy so they can get more engagement. Meanwhile the world is burning. People would feel betrayed and turn on me with unmitigated rancor if there was a photo published of me smoking a cigarette. It's that exacting. How could anyone not become paranoid? And on the flip side, as I'm sure you have experienced, there are also people who will defend to the death the most mediocre white men who could be accessories to war crimes for all they care.

'The world is on course for catastrophe, and I'm worried about whether or not I've been sufficiently polite to someone who asked me for directions when I was not paying attention. Meanwhile there are people boarding the tube with alligators and boa constrictors and everyone is telling me that no one even notices. I think I notice a lot about strangers. Usually at a glance I feel like I can reconstruct where they're coming from, where they're going. It's not something I think about consciously or something that I even try to do, I just receive the information. I used to think I was so clever, that I knew so much, that I was going to be able to change.

Something that is very effective in getting me to calm down is thinking about the vastness of the cosmos and the oddness of the physical universe. Most of everything is made of nothing. Contact is an illusion created by interactions between negatively charged electrons. Connection is literally repulsion. When you think about that, when you consider that sitting on a chair right now you're being held up by particles that you're not really touching—that nothing might be what it seems on the most basic physical level, what certainty can you have about anything else? I find that comforting.'

'You find uncertainty comforting?' Autumn wondered. She had been taking notes and flipped back a few pages.

Layne nodded. 'I think so.'

'How often would you say that you get stuck thinking about the same thing for hours?'

'I'm not sure. Often. Definitely often. I wish that wasn't how my mind worked.'

'Have we discussed the possibility of "pure obsession" OCD?' Autumn asked.

Layne shrugged. 'Probably, but I think we got distracted by something else.'

'Do you experience any physical compulsions or rituals?'

'You know I do. You've seen me turn my phone on and off for upwards of twenty minutes.'

'Do you think these sessions are still helpful to you? Do you think maybe you should be seeing someone else. I'm doing my best, but if I'm perfectly honest I have been thinking of you more as a friend than as a client.'

'As a friend?' Layne was baffled. Where was this coming from?

'Do you want to grab coffee on Tuesday? Also, did you know that I'm really good on electric bass?' Autumn's smile reminded Layne of a cat that had just managed to knock over a bottle of cream.

'Well, I've been thinking we'd like to take some of our stuff heavier,' Layne said, trying to entertain the possibility. 'We could use a bassist.'

'Going back to the body in the car park—'

Layne grimaced. 'Do we have to?'

Autumn leaned forward, intrigued by this reaction 'Why do think you would like to avoid talking about it?'

Layne shook their head in disbelief. 'Because you want to take charge of a murder investigation. I'm not enabling that.'

'Enabling? You think you have a responsibility to keep me in check? That is very interesting.' Autumn made a note on her legal pad. Layne blinked at her, not quite believing what they were seeing.

'I thought we had sort of established that you're not my therapist anymore,' Layne said, hoping they had not somehow consigned themself to being the subject of a podcast episode.

'The question still stands,' Autumn said patiently. There was no trace now of the excitable consumer and re-teller of lurid narratives. She appeared every inch the trusted, collected confidant. She could have been asking out of genuine concern.

Layne raised an eyebrow to Autumn, trying to assess what she was playing at, and then looked glumly down at the rug. 'Because I want to be in control of the narrative, and I don't want you picking apart what I'm trying to do and psychoanalyzing it.'

'What if I promise not to say anything?' Autumn offered. 'Would you talk about it then? If I promise to just sit here silently?'

'It doesn't make a difference. I know you would still be mentally dissecting everything I'd say, and I haven't decided yet what I actually want the narrative to be,' Layne said, hoping that somehow this would give Autumn enough to chew on that she would stop pressing the subject.

Instead, Autumn made another note on the legal pad. 'The narrative of discovering the body?'

Layne realised they may have now gone too far to be able to turn back. Autumn had gotten some kind of answer out of them. They may as well attempt to clarify the situation. 'I know it sounds crazy, because I wasn't actually the one who discovered him and it's not like there are any kinds of weird nondisclosure agreements or anything like that. It's not really my story to tell. No part of it is really my story and yet I'm trying to twist it to my own ends even when I'm not even quite sure what those ends are yet.'

Autumn looked at Layne for a long time. She was clearly worrying about something, but she did not seem to be worried about Layne. There was a more immediate concern than the psychological knots Layne had just laid out in front of them. Finally, she asked 'Do you personally think it was a murder?'

Layne slid their hands into the pockets of their jacket. 'I could lie to you.'

'Please don't?' Autumn said plaintively.

Layne didn't say anything for a moment. If this was about to turn into a murder investigation, Autumn would want to get involved and Autumn was an unaccounted for variable. Autumn would spin the narrative in her own direction and Layne was not confident that they would necessarily be able to maintain any influence on what that direction was going to be. But if they were to lie, there was no way Autumn would believe them and it would only make everything more complicated.

'Yes,' Layne said finally. 'I think Robert Douglas was murdered.'

Autumn set down the notebook. It could have been a gesture indicating that they were off the record, but Layne knew better. If anything, Autumn was giving herself more leeway to embroider the narrative. 'Was there an autopsy?' Autumn asked.

Layne shrugged. 'There was. I obviously did not receive any details beyond what was officially reported.'

Autumn took this in as something of a reality check. Of course, Layne would not have heard any more than anyone else—

she was not sure why she had assumed that she would have. Apparently being a rockstar didn't give you all the keys to the kingdom. Or access to confidential records, for that matter.

'What makes you think it was a murder?'

'Besides your own unshakeable conviction that foul play was involved?' Layne scrutinized Autumn suspiciously, wondering what other kind of scrutiny there were.

'My conviction is far from unshakeable,' Autumn said gravely. 'I started out by asking what you thought had happened.'

'If you must know, I think there is more to Robert's death than it appears because of how his brother reacted,' Layne explained.

'What about how he reacted?'

'He was shocked. Really genuinely shocked."

'I thought they didn't know each other very well. I thought they were estranged.'

'They were, but I feel like he knew enough to—' Layne trailed off, not sure what they were trying to say.

'How would he know if Robert had been murdered?'

'He wouldn't. But he would know how likely it was that he would die.'

'Did Alan collect any life insurance?'

'There was no life insurance. No insurance and no will.'

'Well, that's a motive gone then,' Autumn said opening the notepad and dragging her pen across a line of text.

'Autumn, for God's sake, this is not a game of Clue.'

'I'm just trying to piece together what happened.'

'Have you played London before?'

'Is that a board game?'

'A concert in London,' Autumn clarified.

'Excuse me?' the change of subject was so abrupt Layne could not be sure they had heard correctly.

'Where else have you played in London?'

'I've played at a few smaller venues. We've opened for some of our friends when they've toured here.'

'Where specifically?'

'Do you think this might be related to what happened to Robert?'

Autumn rested their chin on their hand. 'Were they clubs, bars, theatres, what sorts of places?'

'Theatres mostly.'

'Interesting.' Autumn scribbled down another note.

Layne had something else they wanted to say. 'One other thing—'

Autumn leaned in, hoping to catch any more details Layne was willing to share. 'Yes?'

'I was wondering if you had any advice on coming out?'

Autumn set down her pen. Layne had not discussed this before. Autumn knew Layne recognized that a large proportion of The Stone Dandelion's fanbase was queer and had made many statements of solidarity over the years.

'On coming out as what to whom?'

'Nonbinary. To everyone, I think?'

'Oh, congratulations.'

'And I've got a new publicist. He's been telling me he's worried about his partner because she's having copyright challenges to her play that just opened on the West End.'

Autumn clicked the end of her pen and considered this dilemma. 'Is it the music? Usually, they just say you can't record the show if there's copyrighted music.'

'No. There isn't music in the play.'

'A play with no music? What kind of a play is that?'

'That's what I thought, but I guess there are a lot of shows that don't have any music. There is sound design, apparently. Some weird atmospheric stuff. I thought it was pretty cool.'

'Have you seen the production?' Autumn asked.

'I was there on opening night.'

'What's it about?'

'I'm not sure it really has an 'about.''

Autumn scratched her head and looked at Layne sort of sideways. 'Has it got characters?'

'I think so.'

'You're not sure?'

'It was all very abstract. There were lots of fragments of monologue and stage pictures. I guess parts of it were sort of like *Love and Information* by Caryl Churchill where you don't realise quite how much work the director did to decide what was happening until you glance at the script. I don't think I quite understood it, but it was definitely very queer.'

'Queer as in gay?'

'Queer as in queer. But apparently there was another play written by some woman in America that had scenes that were the same.'

Autumn nodded, pretending to understand. 'I'm sure that happens all the time. People have similar experiences and want to explore similar themes.'

'I don't mean that they were similar. Richard said the text of the scenes was exactly the same as a couple scenes from this other play. But apparently the style of that play was quite different. A lot more realistic. Or there was…more realism…in the play, however you want to say it. It was about a queer student's experience on a high school swim team. The sort of thing you would expect one of the regional theatres to pick up. Only I don't think any of them did.'

'Was it any good?'

Layne shrugged. 'I don't know. I haven't read it. But there are a couple of scenes with a young student in Shamira's play. Those were the ones that were exactly the same.'

'Are we talking a couple of lines?'

'Apparently. But they were really specific.'

'That's not a good look.'

'No,' Layne agreed.

'So, your publicist is trying to sort that out?'

Layne made a noncommittal noise, the sort you make when you don't really want to say no. 'Not really. He just told me about it.'

'Do you think he has the skills to handle that kind of crisis?'

'If someone sued me for copyright infringement?'

'Or the other way around.'

'I think so, from a PR standpoint, he can be quite professional.'

'So, his girlfriend stole scenes from someone else's play.'

'She didn't steal them.' Layne objected. 'Richard thinks it's a coincidence.'

'I see.'

'I don't think it can actually have been a coincidence,' Layne said, going back on what they had just said.

'Neither do I,' Autumn agreed.

'She may have remembered the text but not remembered where she remembered it from,' Layne considered.

Autumn nodded. 'And then when she went to google the lines nothing turned up so she figured she must have thought of it herself and thought maybe she was experiencing déjà vu.'

'Has she done anything in America, this Shamira Allis?'

'Not that I know of.'

'Maybe there was an online writer's group? Or playwrights shared their work through direct messaging on social media? Ms. Allis could very well have this other play saved on her hard drive.'

'You think so?'

'I think it's by far the most likely scenario,' Autumn said with great gravitas.

'Just like you're certain that Robert Douglas was murdered?' Layne asked.

'In terms of sheer probability? Absolutely.'

Chapter Six. Golden Dreams

Layne Thompson had given an interview shortly after they landed at Heathrow. Jet-lagged and sleep-deprived they clutched the large cup of coffee they had bought on the way out of the airport.

Layne's first impression of the woman interviewing them was that she was much cooler than Layne was. Fortunately, they were too exhausted to have any opinions about this. She looked at Layne over the top of her cat's-eye plastic rimmed glasses and her jacket was some kind of tweed-like material that Layne could not imagine ever getting wrinkled. She offered Layne an insulated paper cup containing a much smaller and more expensive cup of coffee than the one Layne had purchased at the Heathrow Caffe Nero. This momentarily threw Layne for a loop, and they stood at an impasse for several seconds before setting down the large coffee on the nearest horizontal article of hotel lobby furniture.

'How was your flight?' the interviewer asked by way of greeting.

'Turbulent,' Layne said, sipping their miniature flat white. It tasted like west London.

'I'm sorry to hear that,' the interviewer said sincerely. 'You're playing London, Brighton, Newcastle, Birmingham, Cardiff, Glasgow and Dublin on this tour, aren't you?'

'And Manchester.'

'And Manchester, of course. What would you say you're most looking forward to?'

'I've spent a lot of time in the UK and Ireland over the years,' Layne said thoughtfully. 'I'm planning on counting all of the sheep that I see through the windows of the van.'

'Will this help you sleep?' There was a hint of a smirk in the interviewer's voice.

'No, if I sleep, I might miss some of the sheep. I need to come up with an accurate number.'

'I'll come back and ask you in a few weeks, shall I?'

'You do that. Expect a number in the high hundreds.'

'So, The Stone Dandelions, where did the name come from?'

'I guess it was the idea of Medusa turning anything she looks at to stone and maybe about what it meant to look at someone versus being looked at. Dandelions are known for scattering seeds to the wind, which they can't do if they are petrified, but also there's also this idea that something so ghostly, so symbolically mortal, could be preserved like a statue.'

The interviewer pressed her lips together skeptically. 'That's a different story than the one you gave the last time you were asked.'

'You want to know the truth? I went online to look up band name generators and it came up in the list the third time I ran the generator. I can give you the link. I saw it and I thought, oh, Rolling Stones, The Stone Roses, Guns 'N' Roses, there might be something there.'

'You're lying again,' the woman observed.

'I didn't come up with the name. It came to our drummer Mila in a dream, and she insisted it had to be the name of the band.'

'Which answer do you want me to print?' The interviewer clicked the recording button on her microphone a couple of times, switching it off and back on again.

Layne shrugged. 'That's not for me to decide, is it?'

'The art on the first album cover is a black-and-white photo of a dandelion in bloom.'

'I took it on a 2005 Nokia camera phone and then changed the colours in Microsoft Word.'

'Is there a reason—'

Layne inhaled contently. They could say whatever they wanted. 'They're edible plants, high in calcium and containing more protein than spinach. Good in salads, good when they're cooked. They have tons of uses, they're bright and sunny but often seen as weeds. Yet kids are encouraged to blow on them to scatter the seeds. There are a lot of different kinds of dandelions. They mutate relatively easily as well. When I'm walking around my hometown in the spring, I often see dandelions with multiple heads growing on a single stalk or multiple stems fusing together to form a single flower. I even saw one that looked like a dozen flowers had melded together on a stalk wider than my arm. Come to think of it, I wonder what that says about the soil and water run-off conditions that those things are happening to the flowers. We might be sitting on some nuclear waste. I never considered that at the time. I just thought that there were so many growing in that lot that some of them were bound to end up like that. I took a photograph of it if you would like to see it?'

Layne brought out their phone and scrolled through the camera roll. After a couple of minutes of flicking their finger across the screen, they found the photo and showed it to the interviewer who stared at it for several seconds. The silvery green stalk of the plant warped and twisted in all directions and at the very top split into multiple heads like a hydra. Their interviewer stared at it, aghast.

'So, do you think you're going to stay in New York?' the interviewer asked, looking at Layne's face rather than their phone screen.

'I've been thinking about this lately,' Layne said as though this were the very first time they were considering the question. 'The city's been hit very hard by global warming. It doesn't get nearly as cold in the winters as it used to, and the summers have become quite genuinely dangerous. It's really very alarming. I suppose it's probably like that in any city that I could move to. I just keep noticing the difference every year. The weather getting more and more extreme.' Apparently realising this did not answer the question, Layne frowned. 'I'll probably stay.'

'Can you tell us a bit about what we might be hearing? A sneak peak of the setlist?'

'We're kind of touring *Evergreen* but we're planning to mix it up. Maybe roll a dice backstage. Or onstage. I've been thinking of bringing out a magic eight ball,' Layne said with characteristic earnestness.

'You seem like you're really interested in entertaining the people who end up reading this interview.'

Layne nodded. 'I'm really interested in entertaining everyone.'

'The truth is rarely pure and never simple, but people can have a nice five minutes waiting at the dentist's office? Is that the idea?' The interviewer asked.

'I'd be very flattered by some random person at a dentist's office deciding to read this interview while they wait.'

'Let me see if I've got any harder-hitting questions.' The interviewer flipped over a sheet of notes and rubbed her chin thoughtfully. 'Are you more afraid of failure or success?'

'Oh, success, hands down. I'm fucking petrified of success. Failure to me has always seemed totally low stakes. If you record a flop no one hears about it. If I sing the wrong notes, I don't think anyone's actually going to hold it against me. If a gig goes horribly there's always the next one. It's when people start having expectations of you that you run into problems. If I have to live up to something or else people are going to be disappointed. That's terrifying. Before I was in this position, before I was where I am now, I had a really hard time respecting my own work.'

'What do you mean by that?' The interviewer was scratching down notes evidently ancillary to the tape recording.

'I would sort of devalue anything I did, anything I was any good at as because if I recognized that I was actually skilled I would have to recognize that there were possibilities that I had never considered and that I could do more than I ever dreamed was possible. What really helped, what really changed things for me was when other people's dreams got wrapped up in my own. Because I could not let my friends down. I could not disappoint them. I love my friends and I would move heaven and earth for them.'

'That's lovely.' The first sincere smile from the interviewer. Layne's subconscious decided to shatter it.

'Or course now fame is just a nightmare. It's an almost exclusively negative experience. Not because of anything specific that anyone has done, just because of how frightened I am of the possibility of people knowing who I am at any minute of the day.'

Instead of shattering, the interviewer's smile twisted into bemusement. 'Not that I'm trying to minimize or dismiss in any way what you're talking about, but have you spoken to many people who live in small towns?'

'Small towns?'

'Because in a small town everyone knows everyone else. I always thought becoming famous would be like more of the world becoming a small town to you.'

Layne shook their head vigorously. 'No, it's not.'

'What?'

'It's not like that at all because there's a power dynamic to it. They know who you are but you don't know who they are. If you live in a small town you know your neighbours. I don't know the people who come up to me and pour their hearts out to me. I'd like to make it very clear that I'm not complaining. I appreciate what they're experiencing, and I care about them. I care deeply about how they're trying to connect with me and how what my friends and I have done has meant so much to them. It just happens to often be more than I can deal with, and I don't necessarily know how to express that to them. Then I get very worried I may have crushed their expectations by not being able to be what they hoped I would be.'

'Well, you've certainly not crushed any of my expectations.' The smile was back.

Layne feigned apology. 'That's very kind of you to say after this interview. I'm afraid I may have somewhat derailed the conversation.'

'Not much more than usual,' the interviewer chuckled lightly.

'What do you mean by that?'

'It's me.' The interviewer said. 'It's me, your publicist. Today I'm going by Violet. Did you really not recognize me?'

'Oh! Thank you for telling me. I mean— I didn't recognize you, we've only met in person a couple of—'

Violet nodded slowly, almost sarcastically. 'I noticed that.'

'Did you— Is that what you want? To be seen differently?'

'I'm the same person.'

Layne thought about this. 'That's not always a given.'

'I know. But yeah. I'm the same. Just a different gender some of the time.' Violet zipped her microphone equipment back into its foam-lined case.

'That's really cool.'

'Is it?'

'I think so. Not that I can actually speak to how anyone else thinks so maybe it depends on what your definition of cool is."

Violet rolled her eyes and then grinned broadly. 'Thank you. I appreciate it.'

'Violet.' Layne pronounced. 'My publicist is named Violet and she has her shit together.'

'I wouldn't say that.'

Chapter Seven. Balm of Hurt Minds

Morgan Garrett tried to listen to the rising and falling susurration of the debate that continued around them. Voices seemed to blend together, weaving in and out of comprehensibility. Some people were incredibly angry, but they were being incredibly polite about it. They were talking over each other and then pausing to shift the topic of the argument to how they would not be able to get anything done if they kept talking over each other. Morgan tried to recall what the debate was originally about but the repeating chorus of 'with all due respect' echoed in their head. Under the intertwining layers of voices, they could hear the hum of the air conditioning. It brought a delicious cool to the room. The air was such a perfect temperature they felt sure that there was no way that what was being discussed at that moment was anything to worry about. The edges of the room in front of them blurred out and they felt everything around them soften. Sometime later they jerked awake, neck aching.

Morgan blinked in the light and the MP sitting beside them glanced at them askance, just noticing for the first time that they had fallen asleep. Then they saw the round oil-on-water gleam of the lens of a television camera.

They recalled someone mentioning that the debate was going to be televised but they hadn't thought much of it, considering that if they featured in any of the footage it would be in brief shots of B-roll panning around the room. Morgan had not expected a sustained shot of them falling asleep to be broadcast on live television.

Morgan leaned over to the person sitting next to them and whispered in his ear. 'What were they discussing?'

'Regulations on CO_2 emissions,' he whispered.

Morgan sat upright and froze in place. A wave of regret washed over them, and the weight of dread settled in their stomach. They would have had something to say. They would have had quite a lot to say. Something awful could have happened in the minutes they had been asleep and now they weren't sure what to follow in the continuing debate. It would look like they didn't care. They had become so used to sweltering rooms and opening all the windows, trying to plug in box fans and laying damp cloth on their skin to try to cool down that spending a couple of hours in an air conditioned room had been so comfortable in contrast that it had lulled them into the placid embrace of sleep. And now it looked like they did not care about the climate crisis. They pictured the flicker of screens as hundreds of people took screenshots of the broadcast. They had been elected a couple of years back. Morgan's track record had been unremarkable. They toed the party line and did not speak up often, so this would probably be the first most people had heard of them besides a couple of articles that had run when they had come out as nonbinary.

For the most part no one had taken any notice of them but now they would be recalled as the backbencher who had fallen asleep during a climate debate. Even then, Morgan doubted anyone would really pay any attention to who they were. They would merely become a symbol of a culture of apathy in the face of impending crisis. In the grand scheme of things, they were more distressed by the broader implications of such a symbol then the fact that they would be its face. Morgan would still have an ordinary, uneventful life and the media storm would soon blow over.

Two weeks later Morgan was sitting on a plastic chair in a concrete hallway waiting to hear their name.

Inside a square grey room which, based on the assortment of furniture inside, now pushed up against the walls or neatly stacked, was sometimes an office and sometimes a classroom, a director and a stage manager sat behind a table. 'Morgan Garrett? Do you think that's *the* Morgan Garrett?' the stage manager asked.

'What?' the director looked up from her notes.

'The politician. Morgan Garrett. The one who fell asleep during a debate in parliament.' The stage manager spoke in bright, urgent tones. He was intrigued by the prospect. No one had really turned on Garrett when the images of them sitting limply with their head lolled forward had circulated. It was the rest of parliament that had been castigated for their lack of urgency. There were even some climate activists who had commented, presumably ironically, that they would have done the same thing if they had been in Garrett's position.

The director did not recognize the name. 'Nah, I doubt it,' she said.

'But they could be, right? Have you got their headshot?' The stage manager reached across the table and rifled through the folder full of actor headshots.

The director rolled her eyes up to the ceiling. This was getting silly. 'Why would an MP be auditioning for a regional tour of a play based on a soap opera?'

The stage manager looked quizzically up at the spot on the ceiling that the director was staring at. 'Didn't they resign?'

'I don't know,' the director was not about to let the stage manager know that she did not know who he was talking about. 'Did you read that somewhere?'

Now the stage manager was uncertain if they were recalling any of the story correctly. 'Yeah,' he said, 'I thought they did.'

There appeared to be a water stain on the plaster of the ceiling. It looked a bit like a cartoon fish blowing a bubble with chewing gum. 'Did they resign out of embarrassment, do you think?'

'A really quiet exit in ignominy and hardly anyone even noticed,' the stage manager said confidently, now completely uncertain whether Morgan Garrett was really the name of the MP who had fallen asleep or if they were getting the incident confused with something else entirely.

The director accepted him at his word. 'Why would they?' she asked, as though politicians resigned every day, which, to her, it seemed like they did.

The stage manager scratched his head. 'Because they were part of the national government?'

The director nodded in distracted agreement. 'That's a good point.'

The stage manager looked back at the folder of headshots. 'Aha!'

'What is it?'

'It *was* Morgan Garrett!' the stage manager exclaimed.

'What was?'

'The politician.'

'Oh. Should we call them in?'

'Oh yes, we should, shouldn't we?'

Morgan stood up when their name was called. They remembered reading an article on how to open doors to create the best impression. They stood in front of the door and tried to remember which hand to turn the doorhandle with. They settled on their left hand, pulled the door open, stepped in front of it, promptly forgot what they were supposed to do next, propped the door open with their foot and then allowed it to close behind them. The director and stage manager watched this little dance without comment.

'Good morning,' Garrett said.

'Hello,' said the stage manager.

'I'm auditioning for the tour,' Morgan said, not knowing what else to say.

'You're a member of parliament,' the stage manager observed as a sort of disjointed corollary from this declaration.

'I was,' Morgan agreed.

'You resigned?'

'I'm quitting politics. I've been a backbencher the whole time, I genuinely think I could make more of a difference in the arts.'

The stage manager glanced at the director, mouth twitching into a half smile. 'As an actor?'

'Actors have a lot of influence. They can sway a lot of people's opinions.'

'Do they now?' the stage manager spoke in a low voice, just dodging deep sarcasm.

'Celebrity culture is a lot more potent than any of us want to believe.' Morgan had thought about this a lot. They had listened to who exactly it was that people talked about when they were discussing different points of view. Politicians were so often written off as a lost cause.

'You don't automatically become famous just from being an actor and you don't automatically get any actual influence just from being famous either,' the stage manager said all in one breath before he could stop himself. So, this was how the MP who fell asleep on camera thought.

'I won't be the first person who has gone into acting to try to change the world,' Morgan said resolutely.

How had they been elected? How had such idealism remained intact to stand in front of two people casting the stage adaptation of a soap opera. 'That doesn't mean it makes actual sense as an actual course of action.' The stage manager said. The director elbowed the stage manager in the ribs to prevent him from saying anything else.

'I'm going to start here.' Morgan planted their feet firmly on the purplish grey carpet 'If I've kept my sense of purpose, I hardly think that's a problem.'

'Alright,' the director said, nodding for Morgan to continue on to their actual audition.

'I haven't memorized my sides, or printed them out, so I'm just going to read the lines off my phone,' Morgan said. It wasn't an apology, or even much of an explanation.

'Just because you're a member of parliament doesn't mean we're going to cast you either.' The stage manager was joking but all this achieved was the director treading on his foot under the table.

'Give me a chance at least, come on,' Morgan said sweetly.

The stage manager glanced back up at the bubblegum-chewing fish on the ceiling. 'Begin whenever you're ready.'

'Thank you.' Morgan closed their eyes and appeared to begin a deep breathing exercise.

The director discretely removed her foot from on top of the stage manager's. He opened his mouth immediately. 'Although we happen to be on the clock, so sooner rather than later would be best.'

'Alright, alright,' Morgan said. 'I'm just thinking over the scene'

The stage manager shot the director a look and shook his head, lips pressed together.

Morgan fumbled with their phone for several seconds and managed to open the pdf they had been sent. 'Yes. You can check whatever box you feel like you need to check,' Morgan read, a little flatly.

'I think you should see a doctor,' the stage manager said, looking levelly at Morgan. The stage manager had a BA in acting from a conservatory. You could tell this from the way that his unadorned line reading sounded like he was answering the phone after having been awakened from deep sleep by his ring tone.

Morgan looked back at their lines on the pdf on their phone screen, found where they were and then coyly avoided the stage manager's gaze. 'I don't like doctors.'

'You said your doctor was really nice,' the stage manager continued.

'Yes, when I was living alone and hadn't spoken to anyone in a week.' Morgan was beginning to get into it now, speaking in a more natural rhythm.

'But she's actually really nice,' the stage manager said evenly. It would be easy to lace some sarcasm or deadpan amusement into his line delivery, but the stage manager was a professional.

'I think that's enough, thank you,' the director interjected cheerfully.

The stage manager jumped a little in his seat as though it were his own audition that were being cut off, half expecting another elbow in the ribs.

'You'll let me know?' Morgan asked, eyes flitting from the pdf to the director. She had cut them off about a third of the way through the first side. They had no idea how typical this was but they had read that directors sometimes cut people off, so they were not going to worry about it.

'We'll let you know if you get the part,' the director said cheerily.

That sounded promising to Morgan, and they left the audition room with a spring in their step.

Chapter Eight. Your Local Two-Screen Cinema

Shamira was juggling five sandwiches in two toaster ovens with one pair of tongs. She had developed a system to do this without thinking about it, it had taken a few months but eventually muscle memory and habit meant she could do this without error while lost in a daydream. The daydream in question involved a garden bathed in golden sunlight filled with herbs and vegetables. In her mind she planted herbs in spirals in the soil, coriander sprawling against mint that she plucked multiple times a day to keep it from overtaking the planter bed. In her mind while she tucked the tag of a teabag into the rim of a cup she was also dropping a handful of bright green leaves into a tall glass and pouring steaming water from a clay pot over them. The garden was surrounded by a wall made of several kinds of stone, a wall that had been ruined and repaired over centuries. She could trace histories of civilizations in the stone. Some of it carried shells and coral from ancient oceans. It was full of archways leading into sun-gilded passages and the garden was open to the sky. Standing in the beam of light from the window of the café, Shamira was also submerged in the otherworldly warmth of the sun that streamed into the garden, soft but with an edge to it, light born in the heart of star.

As she handed the mint tea and bags of sandwiches across the counter, she was gazing into the convection patterns below the surface of the sun, tracing helium as it made its hundred-thousand-year journey through the body of the star. She envisioned the areas hotter and cooler plasma driving the churning and shifting of the blazing heart that fed most life on Earth.

'You're the kid who got a West End transfer.' The person speaking to Shamira was not the one who had ordered all the sandwiches. She blinked, seeing a little more of the plastic tables and plastic wall art of the café and a little less of quantum-tunnelling high-speed protons.

'From Camden Fringe,' the teenager at the counter continued. They were wearing a tattered hoodie with the logo of a band Shamira thought she recognized. 'The really gay one. Sorry. I mean the play was a really lucid depiction of the queer experience. Especially what it's like to find community through chance meetings and how quickly people are willing to share their— Sorry, I've probably had too much coffee already, should I start over?'

'Um. Yeah,' Shamira said. 'I mean I am Allis. Shamira Allis. You're correct,' Shamira picked up a rag from a tray of disinfectant and wrung it out. It stung her skin, but only a little.

'My brother bought the program at Camden Fringe and then I saw the posters in the tube.'

'We've got posters in the tube?' Shamira dropped the rag back into the disinfectant. 'Which line?'

'Central Line. In the corridor on the way to the exit in Bank.'

'Really?' to have a poster for a play she had written put up in an underground station had been a dream of Shamira's for as long as she could remember.

'Why'd you end up changing the title?' the person across the counter asked.

'Changing the title?'

'From *Those Flowers Might Be Ours* to *These Flowers Might Be Ours*?'

Shamira looked up in surprise. 'Do you know, I think you might be the first person to have picked up on that. The reviewers certainly haven't.'

'They haven't?' the kid asked as though this was the most expected thing in the world. 'I would have thought that would have been one of the first things they would have commented on. It's like a free paragraph of analysis of the meaning of the show.'

Baffled by the layers of sarcasm at play, Shamira asked, 'You think a one-letter change is a paragraph of analysis?'

They nodded. 'Absolutely.'

'Look, I'm very flattered and all, but did you actually order a coffee?'

'Shamira Allis is a megacorporate shill?' the kid scoffed. 'They're right when they say never meet your heroes.'

Shamira, who had never been called anyone's hero before, recoiled as though stung.

'I'm joking. I'm sorry. That was a joke.'

'I just get a bit confused.' Shamira retreated behind the pastry display. 'I wouldn't want you to be waiting on coffee because I forgot to get it for you.'

'Do you forget things often?' the kid demanded. 'I'm not trying to be rude, I'm just fascinated by the mechanism of forgetting because I don't really forget anything.'

Shamira blinked. 'You don't forget anything?'

'Not really. I might accidentally not do something I was supposed to do because I had gotten distracted, but I don't actually forget. I pretend to forget sometimes because I think it freaks people out. They don't understand how I can remember conversations that happened years ago or they're disturbed that I can word-for-word recount things that I have heard. I say sometimes that if I don't remember something it's because I never took noticed in the first place, not that I have forgotten it.'

'I'm very sorry but I have to go back to the ovens now,' Shamira said, as politely as she could manage.

The kid nodded, apparently not listening. 'It's not the best. Being able to agonize over things that happened years ago as though they just happened. I cannot say I recommend it.'

Shamira had already turned her back, but she glanced back over her shoulder. 'I can imagine. Have a nice day.'

More orders came through for toasties and paninis and Shamira imagined the slow blossoming of tomato flowers on vines climbing planks carefully tied together with twine and then how the petals would gradually wither and drop into the soil. In her mind's eye she watched the tomatoes grow like a time-lapse video, becoming red and gemlike and scenting the air like summer distilled. Then she pictured the actual fields and greenhouses, the hurried harvest by underpaid, overworked hands, the actual factory where the sandwiches were assembled and the actual freezers in which they were frozen for transport. She put the sandwiches in the oven, once again unnerved by how easily what she was doing, organizing food, picking it up and pressing a button or operating an espresso machine could be automated and accomplished by a robot. The fact that the shelf in the oven was at exactly the right height and the tongs exactly the right shape and the general sense that everything about what she was doing had been modified by thousands of iterations of trial and error made her feel like her job was busy-work, an excuse to fill her time where technology would be more efficient.

If everything had not fit together quite so well, was not quite so user-friendly she would have felt much less alienated. It was not as though she had not sustained burn scars from the oven doors or molten cheese, it was not as though she did not get yelled at by her manager for moving too slowly. She did like speaking to customers and her co-workers. She especially liked when everyone got too distracted thinking about something like whether or not the new restaurant across the street was a tourist trap or whether or not they were allowed to play a playlist consisting entirely of musical theatre songs.

If Shamira was totally honest, she would have expected to make more money from having a play on the West End. She knew theatre was not where the money was, but somehow in her mind's eye she had pictured that if by some stroke of fortune she ended up with a play on the West End she would feel financially secure enough that she could spend her time writing rather than making lattes. But, she considered, it was pretty good research. The café was in a high traffic area, so new people came in every day. She occasionally felt faintly envious of the people who would come in and work on laptops, especially if they came in with headphones on.

Her co-workers were *very* into musical theatre. They assumed she would be as well, what with all the theatre. Shamira had never particularly been into musicals at all. Something about them felt over-polished and underdeveloped. Like there were not quite enough ideas to fill up the two hours and so the writers had decorated their thoughts with lots of motivating piano and repeating melodic motifs that made Shamira feel like the whole production was one long song. There was, however, something fun about listening to showtunes without any context and making up a narrative about what might be happening. Imagining who the characters could be without knowing who the writer had decided they were and what they were supposed to represent. She could make the backstories and environments in her imagination as intricate as she liked without being bound by any constraints of actually knowing what the character was singing about. But her colleagues had been banned from playing the corporate-approved showtunes playlist for the past five months due to customer complaints.

Evidently people coming in to grab a cup of coffee were not interested in hearing three baristas give a passionately performed rendition of a musical revue of Broadway hits. Shamira felt like a cynic for not joining in the singalong with the same wild abandon as her colleagues when the manager was away, but she had never downloaded an original cast album and did not know most of the words. She still joined in as best as she could on the chorus.

That day was not a musical theatre day. It seemed to be making a gradual transition from being an acoustic covers day to being an ABBA day. After meeting Layne and Kiran of The Stone Dandelions, Shamira had paid more attention to how the music she heard was put together, how songs created different energies and atmospheres. She had tried to gain more confidence in her singing, but had come away with the impression that she was not among life's naturally musically gifted. That was alright, because Shamira knew that not everyone saw shifting, glistening visuals associated with every piece of music they ever heard. Not everyone instantly came up with at least three music video concepts for any pop song that came on the radio. Shamira wondered sometimes what she would have had to do differently in life to be able spend the afternoons sketching storyboards rather than steaming soya milk.

Her co-worker, Jayden tapped her on the shoulder. 'I have news.'

Shamira nearly dropped the vanilla mocha she was making. 'What is it? What's happened?'

'So, you know how Cathryn is the way that she is?' Jayden asked.

Shamira set the drink down on the counter. 'Yeah,' she said.

'So, it turns out that if we increase sales by ten percent compared to the previous year, she gets a bonus from the company that doubles her salary.' Jayden's expression was grave.

'What, actually?' Shamira made a gesture indicating that if she had still been holding the cup she would have dropped it.

'Well, it's more like a sliding scale,' Jayden explained, 'but one end of that scale doubles her salary.'

'I don't suppose *we* get any benefit if we increase sales by ten percent.'

'She says we'll get a pizza party.'

'A pizza party?' Shamira pronounced. 'What are we, seven?'

Jayden laughed. 'That's what I thought when she said it.'

'Ridiculous.'

'She also says she will yell at us less,' he continued. 'Do we believe it?'

'Not at all.' Shamira sighed heavily. 'Double her salary? That's mad. No wonder she's been harping on the ten percent number.'

'It's an absurdly massive jump. Think of how many more orders that would be per day. We're already juggling four at once at basically all times. There's always a line. There's only so much we can speed up. There are only ever three of us working at a time.' Jayden expertly rearranged the cups under the milk steamer and espresso machine as he spoke.

'It's not possible.'

'Yeah, it shouldn't be possible, but that's the thing, we've been doing it, we've been increasing sales by ten percent.' Jayden handed two more cups down the bar.

'She thinks she's transformed everything but in reality, she's just getting on everyone's nerves and not doing anything herself.' Shamira glanced at the door as though Cathryn might walk in at any moment. "Oh, that makes me furious. I understand where she's coming from, because who wouldn't want twice as much pay, but that makes me so angry.'

Jayden shrugged, outlined by the sun streaming through the window. 'She's not really the one we should be angry with, though, is she?'

'She is actually the one who's treating us horribly because she's trying to get us to accomplish an impossible task.'

'Which we have done because we're terrified of her. It is incredibly unfair, but it's the company we should be mad at,' Jayden argued. 'They're the ones who gave her this goal to strive for,' he pointed out.

Shamira thought about this. 'What if we made sure it didn't happen?'

'She would just yell at us and lecture us and make us feel stupid and threaten to fire us.'

Shamira sighed. 'I know. It's awful. Thank you for telling me!'

'Yeah, absolutely.' Jayden stepped behind the register to take a customer's order and Shamira thought about what the pile of coffee beans she was staring into would have looked like when they were still growing on the tree and wondered when the trees had been planted and how much forest had been cut down to make room for the coffee to grow.

Late that afternoon, the rain came on suddenly. The clouds churning across the sky were a grey so deep it was nearly purple, and they moved like a huge ladle was reaching down through the heavens to find the perfect cup of broth. It rained harder than expected, drops thudding onto the pavement swift and forceful as the water pressure in a posh hotel room.

Watching the rain run down the windows of the train, Richard was brought back to his childhood, spending hours watching raindrops chasing each other down the glass in his parents' front door, tracking when they would pause and when they would merge together and speed up on their curved path racing towards the bottom of the window. He stared, transfixed at the way light reflected on the surface of the drops, sometimes seeming to split and reflect something different from the colours around the window. No one ever seemed to find it particularly odd that he was content to stand there for hours, although sometimes people asked if he was waiting for something. They just seemed to be glad that he was quiet and not bothering anyone.

The acceleration of the train peeled the drops from the glass, and they vanished glittering into the dark.

Richard was used to feeling confused and left out, mostly because he did not know what questions to ask much of the time. He wondered, sometimes, if people assumed that he knew more about what was happening then he actually did. He was skilled at pretending that he knew what was going on, likely due to a deep fear of being perceived as incompetent. He had no problem with asking people to fill him in on what he did not know, but it was far from intuitive for him to realise what were the right questions to ask to get to know what he thought he wanted to know or to even to pick up on what it was he was missing in the first place.

Chapter Nine. Finding Hecadiah

Ash cradled their phone in their hand. They felt a little bit like the way they felt when they reached out and touched the lighting ball at the natural history museum, seeing the pink and blue lighting attach to their fingertips and feeling energy prickle across the back of their neck, the faint smell of ozone sharpening the air. They had danced their fingers across the surface of the sphere, feeling the layer of charge on the surface of the glass. They were alert and connected and dazzled. They stood up without thinking about it, too much energy fizzing in their bones.

Ash switched their phone screen off, turned it face down on the table and paced from one end of the room to the other. They couldn't believe it. Then it hit them. The reality of what they had just read. A different feeling took over, a floating, dizzy feeling, like the moment before slipping under anesthesia. That was when it hit them that they were far too invested. They had never felt this way about anything before.

Layne had made a post, a screenshot of a typed out and formatted paragraph explaining how they felt about their gender identity and their relationship to the transgender community. Ash had long suspected, though they would only ever have said so jokingly, that Layne Thompson might be nonbinary. To see that Layne felt comfortable enough and supported enough to say so where the world could see made Ash feel as though they were wrapped in something warm, and their body could relax.

Picking up their phone again they quietly read the post out loud while continuing to pace from one end of the room to the other. It was screenshots from a word processer. White text on a black background.

I have always felt connected to the trans community, and I feel like recently a lot of things have fallen into place for me and I am really getting to know my real self, better than I ever had before. I have seen so much comradery and solidarity among transgender and nonbinary fans of The Stone Dandelions and I hope my love and support over the years has been felt. I've been thinking a lot about how I want

to say this, but I've reached a point where I want people to know this about me. I'm nonbinary and I go by they/them pronouns. I love you all and I want you to know that you're not alone.
– Layne XOXO

Ash felt like they could tell that Layne was terrified when they had written this paragraph and had posted it quickly before fear could get the better of them. At least Ash knew that was how they would have felt if they were in Layne's place.

They switched their phone screen off again and took a box of spaghetti out of a cabinet and considered breaking it in half to fit into the pot on the stove. While they were bending the pasta to test its tensile strength, their phone rang. They had kept the default ringtone for fear of attaching an even more intricate web of associations to any song they might choose to use as a ringtone.

They answered the phone and nearly dropped it when they heard who was calling.

Fifteen minutes earlier, Layne was standing next to the hotel room desk, flipping through a physical telephone directory, scanning for a name.

'I didn't know they still made those,' Mila commented.

Layne gave her a bored, disbelieving look and then continued running her finger down the list of surnames beginning with 'P.'

'Alright, I was just trying to say what someone would say if they were in an action movie.'

'Maybe they put a phone number in the letter they wrote?' Kiran suggested. 'Or the letter before that? Or the one before that?'

Layne paused. 'Do we have the letter?'

'Well, no, but—'

'No more pointless suggestions, please.'

'I'm sorry,' Kiran protested. 'I was just trying to be helpful.'

The room descended into silence once again. Then an ambulance passed by outside, siren blaring. The silence was tense. Mila didn't want to know what Layne would do next if they weren't able to get in contact with Ash.

'I welcome actually helpful suggestions,' Layne conceded. 'I just think it might help if you thought before suggesting something.'

'Alright? I said I was sorry.'

'Don't push it, Kiran.'

Kiran threw up her hands. 'What did I do?'

Layne sat down on the bed, examining the directory with increasing frustration. 'What do people have to do in order to be listed in this?'

'I think they have to give them their number? Or was it that you had to request to not be listed?' Kiran frowned.

Mila took in the breadth of the directory and the number of colour-coded sections it was separated into. 'Have you checked the business section?'

'They're a teenager,' Layne reminded her.

'Also, if they have a business, wouldn't it be easier to find online?' Kiran said.

'Maybe Ash isn't their legal name?' Mila offered.

Layne looked from Mila to Kiran and then flipped to the business section.

'I'm going to go through the entire phonebook,' Layne declared with grim resignation. They flipped through the business section at random. They levelled a stare that was almost a glare at their bandmates. 'Unless you have any idea what they might be selling?'

'Shamira said they were wearing a lot of bracelets,' Mila remembered. 'Sort of rubber band kind of things.'

'Shouldn't you be looking for an online shop?' Kiran suggested again. 'No one even has a landline anymore.'

Layne continued flipping at random and then froze. 'You cannot be serious.'

'What?' Kiran asked.

'What is it?' Mila leaned over Layne's shoulder to see what they were looking at.

Layne traced their finger under the line of text on the page. 'Private consulting detective,' they read. 'The kid is a consulting detective.'

'It's gotten very film noir all of a sudden, hasn't it?' Mila giggled. 'This is incredible.'

'Do you think they put this in the phonebook as a joke?' Layne was trying not to laugh.

'Think about it, though. If you had a photographic memory, wouldn't you try to be Hercule Poirot?' Mila said.

'If I had a photographic memory,' Layne said, 'I would learn thousands of songs and record covers for TV shows direct-to-master in one take.'

'I don't think that's how a photographic memory works,' Kiran said.

Mila pulled out her phone. 'Are you going to call them, because if you're not, I'm going to.'

'Should really I be the one to call?' Layne wondered.

'You know you should, but if you don't want to, I will,' Mila's hand hovered over her phone screen.

'Shouldn't it be Violet?' Layne asked.

'What? Because Violet's Shamira's girlfriend? Because she runs social media accounts? No!' Mila crowed.

Mila was about to finishing dialing the number when Layne shook her head. 'No, you're right, I've given Violet a chance to be more involved and she hasn't been interested.'

Kiran twisted her face into an odd expression, brows frowning, lips smiling. 'A chance to be more involved? I don't think Violet is even aware that you're conducting a murder investigation. I don't think Shamira has actually told her.'

'What?' Layne stared at Kiran.

It was true that Shamira had not talked much about Violet after stepping in to suggest that Ash could help after Ash had figured out what had happened with her play. But it had never occurred to Layne that Violet might not have picked up on the fact that there was a major unofficial investigation being spearheaded by her own employer.

'Make the call or I'm going to,' Mila held up her index finger meaningfully.

Layne dialed the number. It was answered on the second ring.

'Ash speaking, how may I help you?'

'You might want to sit down,' Layne cautioned.

'Who is this? Did something terrible happen? Is someone in hospital?' The unspoken additional question of *did someone die* was implied in the moment of silence that hung on the end of Ash's sentence.

'This is Layne Thompson.'

Chapter Ten. Total Eidetic

The afternoon Ash set out to meet The Stone Dandelions, they caught sight of their reflection in the window of a parked car on the side of the road. They looked young and ordinary. Since they were in college, they didn't have to wear a school uniform anymore but the years of being prescribed what to wear meant they had not yet figured out how they wanted to dress for themselves. They had tried wearing skirts and men had shouted at them. They had tried wearing patterns that didn't go together and people shook their heads at them in the hallway. It had been a few days since they had done laundry so they were dressed in sweatpants and a jumper, which they would never in have worn to see The Stone Dandelions play but right now they didn't especially care how they looked.

It was strange to be presented with the prospect of actually getting to know someone who had become a sort of imaginary friend over the years. Ash had had dozens of imaginary conversations with Layne about what it was like discovering the Dandelions music and watching it become a soundtrack to their life. Telling Layne about all the things that happened on nights when they had stayed up for album drops. The night the dog ran away and Ash was able to coax her back by singing to her. The night Ash's mother had lost her car keys but was able to remember where she had put them based on what lyrics she had heard coming from the speakers in Ash's room when she had set them down.

When Ash was younger, they had a difficult time listening to rock music because they found all the sounds overwhelming. The sound would ricochet in their head for hours afterward, gouging out an impression of itself.

Music for Ash often became strongly associated with the place and circumstance where they had first heard it. When they thought of a song they could immediately see the room or area around them where they had first encountered it. If a song had come on in the supermarket, for instance and then they were reminded of it, they could read the row of soup cans that had been in front of them. They didn't have to think about this, or actively remember, the other places and times were simply summoned before their eyes, one thought interlinked with another.

Ash had been going to concerts for years and they enjoyed a mosh pit. Half the time they started out in front of the stage they ended in the middle of the floor, not able to see anything but having the time of their life, feeling flooded by collective energy and enthusiasm. There were actually not that many artists that they would rather stay immediately in front of the stage for. It seemed like it would defeat the point of being there surrounded by so many people who were just as enthusiastic as they were. But it did depend on the kind of show. If the pit was calm and people were not moving around that much, they liked being able to see.

The Stone Dandelions were one of the few bands with larger followings that Ash would be willing to wait around for to get a good spot. It was mostly because they talked between songs and sometimes came up with elaborate stage antics. Even Mila the drummer would talk between songs. She had a mic taped to her face expressly for that purpose which Ash had always found amusing and endearing. Mila, Kiran and Layne played off each other like a comedy triple act which was something Ash had never seen from a band in quite the same way before. Especially because only some of their songs were comedic. If they had been a comedy band that would be another matter, but the core and heart of what they did, The Stone Dandelions took themselves very seriously which was part of what made them so hilarious. They were well known for being a bit dorky and nerdy which was a lot of the reason that Ash felt like they were able to relate to them and their music. Having watched many videos of Dandelions concerts before ever going to see them and laughing hysterical at their antics alone in their room, what had taken Ash by surprise the first time they had gone to see them was their stage presence.

The Stone Dandelions were much cooler in real life than they were on the internet. Ash supposed it was a similar sort of phenomenon to when you saw actors who played so-called ordinary-looking characters on television in real life, and they turned out to be devastatingly attractive. What seemed dorky and unpolished and un-fakeable onscreen seemed like a brilliantly executed, thoroughly thought out performance, even if the details themselves all occurred in the moment with an element of randomness. Layne and Kiran also moved around a lot more than it seemed like they did on recordings. They seemed to run all over the stage, full of uncontainable energy that they had to release in sheer kinetics. Layne seemed much more poised and choreographed, much more like they actually knew what they were doing when they were dancing than the ragdoll cat the internet liked to compare them to in thousands of memes and drawings.

Ash was floored. The performance was a perfectly pitched powerhouse and Ash immediately started saving to buy another ticket to see them again. Every performance they saw subsequently was different, bringing an entirely different mood and energy. Ash felt as though they could keep watching these concerts forever and never get bored. *The Stone Dandelions* were also relatively prolific, averaging a new studio album every couple of years so Ash could see themself having something new to dive into for a very long time if they kept up this pace. They did not know all that much about music production and wondered vaguely if this rate of writing and recording was sustainable. They didn't just stay in the same territory in terms of their sound either, the albums had decidedly different energies from each other and within the albums there was considerable variation in musical style. If someone was determined to pigeonhole the Dandelions into a genre they probably could, they had a lot of pretty simple punk instrumentation on many of their songs and they could have quite a lot of shouting and attitude, there were also quite a few tracks were the guitars got very self-interested and shoegaze-y. It was definitely 2000s-inflected rock music, there was no denying that, but there was a lot of appetite for that kind of thing these days. Their more upbeat songs always managed to raise Ash's mood and could almost always get them to dance. They loved the way fast and driven sound made them feel. They had tried to bring earplugs to wear at the concerts, but every time the opening notes started they had taken them out of their ears because they wanted to feel the sound all the way into the marrow of their bones. They knew they were doing damage to their hearing and kept telling themselves that at the next show they would keep the earplugs in.

When they went to see other bands, they were very conscientious about wearing hearing protection and not standing too close to the speakers, which felt a bit like they were being unfair but they always had an excellent time and so they did not worry about being unfair if it meant they were preserving some of their hearing.

Sometimes Layne picked up a guitar to play rhythm guitar while they sung. Ash always thought it was cool when artists were able to pick up and put down a guitar in the middle of a song, while they were performing. Some could not do it at all and some really struggled with it but Layne did it with a flourish.

At some point, amidst all these concerts Ash was attending, they had to admit to themself that they were attracted to the band members, and especially attracted to Layne. This also felt unfair, but they could not help how they felt. After all, a lot of people felt that way about Layne Thompson, they were an exceedingly attractive person. So, it may have been unfair, but at least it was normal, and that was alright. If they really got carried away, they could buy posters and put them up on the walls of their bedroom. That was a normal thing to do and that was okay. Ash sometimes had to remind themself that they were allowed to like normal things. They had created such a persona for themself growing up as someone who was odd, someone who didn't fit in and took people be surprise because they didn't do what was expected of them that when they did take up an activity that was considered ordinary, such as attending concerts, or having a crush on a famous person, this also took people by surprise and was commented on as though it were even stranger than doing something that no had ever done before. Ash was still trying to process that and decide whether it meant anything besides the fact that people had decided that they were someone they wanted to laugh at and if Ash wanted to make the best of it, they had best decide to laugh along.

Ash felt like Layne may actually be weirder than they were but somehow had acquired a somewhat mainstream following by appealing both to the actual weirdos and to the people who aspired to be weirdos. Ash felt no sense of anything proprietorial about this state of affairs, but they did worry about the extent of their para-social feelings toward Layne. They had read a bit about para-social relationships with fictional characters and youtubers, and their correlation with mental illness and loneliness. It was often said that the secret to happiness was good health and a poor memory and Ash had always moderated alright health and an impervious memory. But they had never known anything different, so they weren't about to allow it to define their happiness just because there were old sayings proclaiming that they were destined to be unhappy. They had, primarily out of curiosity considered trying to use hypnosis to forget something but they could never decide what it was they would try to forget. It always felt like it would be unfair to their memories. Ash did worry sometimes if they had an over-sensitive or poorly calibrated sense of unfairness given the sheer quantity of things that made them worry that they were being unfair. But they did enjoy things deeply, passionately with the whole of their being, which also worried them sometimes because if they went off something or discovered that someone who had created something they had enjoyed had done something they objected to they could go just as far in the opposite direction, which also made them worry that they were being unfair.

So, Ash loved The Stone Dandelions to the maximum degree that it was possible for anyone to love The Stone Dandelions. This could prove problematic but perhaps a clear head would prevail. Ash had always felt like they had a clear head. Sometimes they wished that they did not. Sometimes they deeply wished that they could give themselves fully over to the present without seeing the past in the present and the present in the future. Sometimes they deeply wished that they could feel like their judgment was clouded. Sometimes they felt like it would be a deep relief. They wondered sometimes what sorts of trouble they would have gotten into by now if they had an ordinary memory. Sometimes they wondered if they really believed hard enough that they could forget they could actually empty moments out of their mind. Sometimes they wished they could write over their memories with new ones like burning over an old CD.

Mostly Ash was worried that Layne Thompson would not like them. That they would be completely disinterested and cold and try to get any interaction they had to have with Ash over with as quickly as possible. They did not think Layne would be cruel or impolite or unprofessional, but the possibility that Layne would be uncomfortable or feel like they were putting themself through a situation that they did not want to be in weighed heavily on Ash's mind. They could imagine Layne Thompson in deep distress, with much more on their mind than they would want to share having to put up with a kid who talked too much and was sure to stumble into saying exactly the things that would annoy them most.

Layne had said they were a key witness to a murder. It must have been a murder that had taken some time. A poisoning. Or a stab wound that had been held in place by something until the victim had ended up somewhere else.

There was an article that had run in the Evening Standard saying Layne had paid for the funeral of a man who was found dead in the Oxford Street carpark. That couldn't possibly be the death Layne was referring to. That would be ridiculous. The article had specified that the death was being treated as unsuspicious. But what else could it be?

The whole situation was so absurd that they stopped walking in the middle of the pavement once again and the person who happened to be walking behind them ran into them and shouted 'Watch where you're going! What are standing still on the side of the road for?'

Ash ignored the shouting man and began walking through the events of the evening of the second of July in their mind's eye.

They had left their family's flat shortly before five in the afternoon. At four they had changed into the outfit they had chosen for the concert, black trousers with tears in the knees and a denim jacket covered in pits. They put on purple lipstick and then rubbed a lot of it off with a tissue, so it just looked like their lips were wine-stained.

They made sure that the front door was locked and then they turned and took the stairs down to street. There were a couple of people walking by on the other side of the road. Ash tried to place the language they had been speaking. At a guess they would say Swiss German. They turned the corner and two women with the wheeled shopping bags that were popular near the large supermarkets were speaking to each other in Trinidadian accents. Ash crossed the road to wait for the bus. It arrived at a time that seemingly bore no relation to the time listed in the timetable. Ash could not make out if the previous bus had run late or the next bus had shown up early. Ash stood on the bus without holding onto anything. They put on headphones and tried to guess which songs the Dandelions were going to swap out on their setlist that night. The bus was only moderately crowded. Some people were bringing their shopping home. There was a group of young women in interesting-looking dresses who were evidently on their way to a party. One of them held an open can of beer with a red and white label.

'No, you're not. You have a hotel room.'

'We're travelling by bus,' Layne insisted.

'That is not the same thing.'

'We haven't got a limousine. The only time I've been in a limousine was when I was going to my high school prom,' Layne said, not entirely truthfully.

Ash was delighted. 'High school prom! Like in the movies.'

'It wasn't like in the movies.'

'Really? What was different about it?'

Layne thought about this. 'I drank a lot of really bad coffee from the buffet and my friend, who identified as a gay man, told me he was attracted to me and a lot of people yelled at him.'

'You see, I don't see how that's fundamentally different from what happens in the movies.' Ash had a queue of questions to quiz Layne about growing up in the United States and their role in the music writing process and what microphones and gear they used. They tried to ask these questions to wait their turn and allow them to focus on the matter at hand. But they still ended up opening up their mouth and asking 'So you can't have used the same mic for the vocals on Evergreen as you did on Everything Ends, right? The shape of the sound is so different.'

'Yeah, the microphone on *Evergreen* actually wasn't available yet when we did *Everything Ends*, when it came on the market, we ended up deciding to go with a much airier sound for that record.'

Violet hailed a cab, wondering if the cabbie was going to ask where he recognized Layne from.

'Have you got a photo of Robert—' Ash was about the ask, and then thought better of it. 'No, I should wait, shouldn't I? Until we get home.'

Layne kept their sunglasses on as they got into the cab and adjusted the flop of the wide brim of their sunhat to better hide their face. There was no comment on this.

Ash told the driver the address, glanced back at Violet and Layne questioningly and then asked, 'Could you put the radio on?'

Lisa Lisa's 'I Wonder If I take You Home' came through the speakers and, if Ash thought about it too hard, threatened to make the moment incredibly awkward.

Ash stared out the window. It really was an incredibly gorgeous day.

Chapter Eleven. In The Study With The Candlestick

There was one response to the post Richard had written and posted on Shamira's accounts. It was from someone named Morgan Garrett. The name was vaguely familiar to Shamira. The message left in Shamira's DMs said 'I auditioned for him. Got some really weird vibes. I'd like to talk about it.'

Shamira tossed her phone to the center of the bed. 'How do I respond to this?'

Richard thought about it. 'Meet for coffee? Maybe?'

'Weird vibes? What are we supposed to do about weird vibes?'

'Possible motive?' Richard suggested.

'Professor Peach in the study with the candlestick for the weird vibes. We've all got weird vibes. That isn't anything to go on.'

'Morgan probably meant he was being a creep,' Richard explained. 'They're probably referring to harassment or bigotry.'

'Why not just say that then?'

'Because it's a big accusation to make. Possible grounds for being charged with libel and they probably haven't fully processed what happened yet, especially if it was only a few weeks ago.'

'Can you really be charged with libel for a DM?' Shamira picked up her phone again. 'Do I tell them he's dead?'

'No!'

'Why not?'

'Because we're trying to keep who knows what under control. That's part of the investigation,' Richard said as though this were obvious.

'I thought Robert was brought on to a production that already had a team.'

'That's what it sounded like, but we don't even know what production he was on!'

'Shouldn't I ask that now?' Shamira wondered.

Richard sat up. 'Yes. Ask what production they auditioned for.'

A couple seconds of typing were followed by the abstractly skeuomorphic whooshing sound of a message sending. 'Well, I asked.'

'Are they online? Can you tell?'

A message appeared. Shamira nearly dropped her phone, then she regained her grip and read it out loud. 'It was for a new play called *Roses and Thorns*.'

The temperature of the room seemed to drop a number of degrees. Finally, Richard stood up and asked, 'Is that the play that they say you—'

'Copied. Yes.'

'Robert Douglas was directing the play that you have been sued for plagiarizing?'

Shamira squirmed and then stopped moving, caught in confusion. 'It...seems like it.'

'You don't think he might have been the one to suggest the lawsuit?' Richard wondered.

'It had never been performed!' Shamira said, dumbfounded. 'We were already on the West End. This is insane.'

'What did Garrett say about meeting to talk?'

'I haven't asked yet. Give me a second.' Shamira's fingers flew across the screen.

'Where do you think the producer found the other play?'

'On a shelf at Boston University? I don't know, do I?'

The message notification sound went off. A ping like a package landing on a metallic surface if both the package and the metallic were in a video game and also imaginary.

'What's the polite way to say, no I don't want to meet you at that particular outlet of that particular coffee chain because it is my place of employment, can we meet literally anywhere else?'

Richard bit back a laugh. 'I was told London could be a deceptively small town. I did not think this was what they meant.'

'There's not even a view.'

'It is open until eight in the evening when almost nothing else around there is.'

'Did you know that we've increased sales by ten percent this year?' Shamira asked.

'Ten percent? That's actually mad.'

'Turns out demand is pretty much continually higher then we can ever keep up with.' Shamira neglected to mention what was happening with the promised doubling of Cathryn's salary.

'You know there's a database of the busiest cafes in the city?'

'Well, I would assume that something like that exists, but I haven't actually encountered it, no.'

'You're near the top of the list.'

Shamira shook her head. 'That makes me feel less crazy. Why on Earth won't Cathryn hire more people?'

'Do you think there are a lot of people around who would voluntarily work for Cathryn?'

'You make a good point.'

'What would it take for you to quit?'

'Not being in a massive amount of debt would help.'

'I'm sorry about that. Really, I am,' Richard was almost pleading.

'It was pretty much entirely your fault.' There was a glimmer of light from Shamira's phone. 'Morgan wants to meet on Wednesday next week. I get off early on Wednesday, but I guess I'll stick around.'

'Couldn't think of another place?' Richard asked.

'Couldn't think of a good enough excuse.'

***

Ash's flat was cluttered in a comfortably lived-in way. There were bottles of cleaning products congregating on the kitchen counter, a collection of candles on the corner of the table, piles of books and papers and pens and unopened bills covering most of the rest of the table. The apartment was dark when Ash unlocked the door.

They adjusted the blinds to let the sunlight in. 'I guess my parents are out. Would you like a cup of tea, or maybe coffee?'

'I'd like some tea,' Layne said.

'How do you take it?' Ash switched on the electric kettle.

'Milk and sugar?' Layne wondered if they had to be more specific.

'You sound like you're not sure,' Ash observed.

'I don't know if you're vegan or dairy-free or anything like that.'

'I'm not,' Ash said, putting the kettle on. 'Can you tell me more about what you saw?'

'I was told afterward that rigor mortis had set in five hours earlier. I didn't see the body for very long. I wasn't allowed in the morgue either, obviously.'

Ash pulled a bag of sugar off a shelf. 'Did you ask to be allowed into the morgue? That's going pretty far, isn't it?'

'I did ask, but I made sure I was giving the impression of a hysterical rockstar,' Layne said with warm professionalism.

'Okay, so we have the time of death, you've got some photographs. Including photographs from when he was alive.'

'I can show you more of them if you would like,' Layne offered.

Steam billowed from the electric kettle. To Violet it seemed like far too much steam compared to the amount of water that had been poured into the kettle. The steam pooled along the underside of the cabinets in white billows and crept up the wall. Violet worried that it might be doing some damage to the paint.

Layne flipped through several photos of Robert Douglas she had found online.

'Hmm,' Ash said, looking closely. 'Did you know I would be outside the theatre hours before the concert?'

'You actually—' Layne paused. Violet was leaning in close to the wall, almost smelling the paint. 'Violet?'

'Paint and wallpaper must absorb all kinds of traces of what happen in the environment. If we find out where Robert was poisoned, we could figure out what they used and maybe how they did it.'

'You and what forensics lab?'

Violet seemed startled by this question and Ash was taken aback. 'Sorry, was I rude?'

Violet blinked a couple of times and then thought to say, 'Don't worry about it.'

'I knew you were outside of the theatre hours early because you actually let Violet into the building,' Layne said. 'You saw she was outside and opened the door.'

'I did not see anyone who looked like—'

'I was Richard at the time. I was wearing a dark green jacket and a hat.'

'Oh. Yes. You had a badge.' Ash turned back to Layne. 'I'm pretty sure that I saw him a few blocks away.'

'Saw who?'

'Robert. Our murder victim.' The kettle finally switched off and Ash brought down a couple of mugs from a shelf. 'This would have been a little over half an hour before he died.'

It occurred to Violet then that she really had no reason necessarily to trust Ash. But, then again, she didn't have any reason to trust Layne either and it had not gotten her in any trouble so far. She accepted the mug of tea that Ash handed her.

'He sort of collapsed against a fence and then was able to stand up again and walk away. I had wondered if maybe he was passing out in the heat or if he was drunk or high or something like that.'

'Half an hour before the reported time of death?' Layne confirmed.

'It was at 17:37.'

'Does it bother you sometimes, remembering everything?' Layne asked.

'I mostly get in trouble when people catch me out lying about having forgotten something. Sometimes I misjudge what other people are likely to remember. Especially on the time scale of a few months. Sometimes I think I should come up with a system to get better at hiding the fact that I remember things like the details of conversations years later. Sometimes I consider being more open and honest about it—'

'That's what I was going to ask,' Violet said.

'But when I am I feel like people are afraid of me, that they're looking at me as something more than or less than human. They also always want to test me, you know, "what was happening on March 3rd, 2014?" And I can usually come up with an answer, but it does get tedious. I also have a lot difficulty re-reading something or re-watching a TV show because my mind tries to fill in the words before I get there so it almost feels like there are two voices speaking at once. I think that's why I like music so much, there is enough structure that my brain does not do that so I can enjoy it.'

'Could you perform a song after one listen if someone asked you to?' Violet wondered.

'I'm not trained as a vocalist. There's more to it than just remembering the words and melody,' Ash explained.

'Which direction did he go after he collapsed?' Layne asked.

'North. Up Poland Street.'

'Do you think anyone else saw him?'

'I'm sure a lot of people saw him. I don't think anyone paid any attention to him. Drunk posh bloke in the middle of the afternoon. If they thought anything about him, they were probably thinking of how to avoid him.'

'So, you would not have any idea of who else to question?' Layne wanted to know.

Ash frowned. They could recall the faces of the other people on the street but they did not think tracking any of them down and questioning them would be helpful. 'Generally, what I want to know is where he went between leaning on that fence and ending up in the car park. Why was he walking through the car park? Did he consume anything in the intervening time? Or had he already been poisoned by that point?'

Violet clinked the inside of her mug with a spoon she had found on the table. 'Are you thinking of somehow getting the credit card records?'

Ash glanced at the spoon skeptically and then gestured with their own spoon. 'Also. Question. You said there was no wallet on the body, no identification? Do you think it was stolen before or after death?'

'That's a good question. On the one hand it's Soho. On the other hand, it's Soho,' Layne quipped.

'Your best guess?'

'Before.' Layne said decisively. 'He was a drunk rich guy. Not paying attention to his surroundings.'

'And we have no actual idea how he died.' Ash shook their head.

'Our drummer is always reading books about mushrooms and things like that,' Layne said seemingly at random.

'I had an uncle like that.' Violet pulled the spoon out of her tea and looked at it closely. It was marked with limescale from being left damp after being washed at some point. She wondered how much lime the average Londoner ingested from the tap water per year. Perhaps it was possible to chemically determine how long someone had been in the city.

'Amanita. Death caps. The poison often used to kill Roman emperors.' Ash's eyes lit up. Somehow this was not disturbing to

Layne. It was the light of beginning to see the path ahead of them. 'Mila would know all the signs. Can we call her?'

'Yeah!' Layne said. They expected Mila to answer right away but the phone rang and then went to voicemail.

Mila's recorded voice in Layne's ear said 'Hi, I'm probably practicing with headphones on, unless I'm practicing without headphones in which case, I really can't hear you.'

'Mila!' Layne spoke into the phone. 'We need your mycological expertise. Call me back.'

Less than a minute later Mila returned the call. 'Did you find shrooms? Who'd you get them from?'

'No, we did not find shrooms. We're wondering what you can tell us about amanita mushrooms.'

There was an intake of breath on the end of the line. 'Oh, not those again. Everyone always wants to talk about death caps. They're not that interesting. There are so many more fascinating mushrooms, for instance, did you know that the largest organism on Earth—'

Layne cut her off. 'It's for an actual reason.'

'Lyrics again?'

'Not lyrics. An actual real-life reason.'

Layne heard the static of Mila breathing into the phone microphone. 'Are you completely sure that you didn't find any shrooms?'

'No. How long would it take for someone to die if they ate death caps?'

'I don't know, probably a couple of days.'

'Days?'

'In most cases. It would depend on how much they ate.'

'Is there an amount where it would happen in hours?'

'It's not likely. Where are you? The middle of Epping Forest? Who died?'

'Only Robert Douglas.'

Layne was sure they could hear Mila shaking her head. 'Him again? Why are you so obsessed with him?'

'He died in front of one of our vans.'

Ash tapped Layne on the shoulder. 'Why did you say hours?'

Mila apparently overheard this. 'Yes, why hours? Most organic poisons are relatively slow acting. It isn't like in the movies.

I suppose there are famous cases like hemlock and belladonna that happen quickly, but that's generally considered the advantage. Making it look like a natural illness.'

'Oh, I see. If Robert had been poisoned days earlier, he probably would not be wandering around like he was ready for a night on the town,' Ash realised. 'But it probably took a while, based on when I saw him. So, it could have been organic. But what are the symptoms. He was shying away from the light. Staggering. He looked flushed. But I thought all of that might just have been from the sun and the heat and alcohol.'

Mila caught some of this and was on high alert. 'Wait. Wait. You met someone who saw Robert before he died?'

'Very shortly before he died,' Layne confirmed.

'Did he seem faint? Like he might lose consciousness? Were there signs of delirium?' Mila asked, serious as anything.

Layne wordlessly handed the phone to Ash.

Ash listened to Mila talk for a couple of minutes and then asked, 'But how can I know for sure that he wasn't just drunk and hungover?'

Ash listened for a couple more minutes. They turned to look at Layne in astonishment. 'She agrees with you.'

Layne nodded. 'She does that sometimes.'

Ash affected a broad Scottish accent. 'There's been a murder.'

Violet set down her mug on the table amid the piles of papers. She could see there was no stopping them now. 'Am I meant to understand how you're getting any of this?' she wondered.

Layne appeared to ignore her. 'Now we have to figure out the when, the where and the who,' they said.

Ash picked up Violet's mug and put it in the sink. They held out their hand for the spoon Violet was holding. Violet looked at their open hand for a few seconds and then, reluctantly handed over the spoon.

Chapter Twelve. On The Point Of A Knife

Shamira typed in the search bar looking through the downloads folder on her computer. She knew there were no files titled 'Roses and Thorns' because she had searched when she first received the takedown letter. It was conceivable that at earlier draft of Lilith Gibson's play had a different title but it had not occurred to her to search for the actual lines that had allegedly been copied until Layne had suggested it to Richard.

She typed in the first line of the third scene. 'Are you always this late to class?' It brought up about a dozen drafts of *These Flowers Might Be Ours* which she thought should hold up in court, but as she scrolled further back through the years she discovered some files that were saved as pdfs. She opened one of them and read, with growing horror, the opening stage direction of an early draft of *Roses and Thorns*. There was no title page, and the document was labelled 'Play Script Draft 3.'

Shamira turned her head away from the computer and covered her eyes with her hand. It was exactly as everyone had warned her. Lilith had sent her a draft as part of a large writer's group they had taken part in around 2017. She had pdfs of early drafts of dozens of plays saved on her computer that she had not looked at in years. She had considered deleting them several times when her computer had nearly run out of storage, but she had never gotten around to it.

Shamira peered through her fingers at the scene glowing back at her. She tentatively reached out to scroll down the page. After about half a page the scene went in a different direction than either the current version of Lilith's play or the fragment that showed up in *These Flowers Might Be Ours*. But those opening moments of the scene were word-for-word identical.

Without being too aware of what she was doing, Shamira slid from her chair to the floor. Violet walked into the room as Shamira was in the process of sliding out of the chair. She had a pretty good guess about what had just happened.

'Did you find a draft? Of Lilith's play?' Violet asked.

Shamira looked up at her balefully. 'What do you think?' Shamira sank to the kitchen floor, expressionless and trembling. Violet approached, kneeling gently beside her. Violet did not think she had ever seen Shamira have a panic attack before, although she had talked about it happening.

'Is there anything I can do to help?' Violet asked, keeping her voice low and calm.

Shamira didn't move. She had her back to a cabinet and her gaze was directed at a spot on the floor in front of her. Violet waited and eventually she shook her head minutely.

'Are you sure?' She asked.

Shamira closed her eyes.

'Do you want me to stay here?' Violet settled more comfortably onto the floor.

Shamira reached for her hand and squeezed it tightly.

'I love you,' Violet whispered. 'I love you, I love you, I love you.'

Violet squeezed her hand back and Shamira rubbed her thumb over the back of Violet's hand. They sat there together on the kitchen floor for a long time. Violet could hear the ticking of a clock from the other side of the wall. She could not remember having heard that clock before. Perhaps the neighbours had bought it recently. Shamira did not move except to occasionally squeeze Violet's hand.

'It's going to be okay. Just keep breathing.' Violet's voice was like a salve, gradually bringing Shamira back to reality.

She leaned against Violet's shoulder and Violet wrapped an arm around her, holding her against her chest. Shamira's heart was beating rapidly but Violet hoped feeling her own steadier heartbeat against her body would physiologically help her calm down.

Shamira sighed. 'Why am I so scared all the time?'

'I did not think that you were,' Violet said.

'It's gotten worse recently.'

'You probably have an anxiety disorder,' Violet leaned back against the cabinet as well.

'I think I don't have enough to focus on. When I don't have something to focus on, I tend to spiral because my energy doesn't have anywhere to go.' Shamira considered.

'You'll have something to focus on soon enough. Your career isn't over, I promise.' Violet rubbed Shamira's shoulder.

'But you can't know that,' Shamira objected, stirring in Violet's arms.

'Yes, I can,' Violet said firmly. 'You are going to have a brilliant career.'

'You can't actually know. Nothing is certain. I could be hit by a bus tomorrow,' Shamira let go of Violet's hand.

'Don't say things like that.'

'I could be blacklisted from the industry. For all I know I already have been.'

'You won't be.' Violet said, 'There would be no actual reason for anyone to turn on you.'

'I can think of ten off the top of my head,' Shamira pouted.

'But the balance of probably is that that's not ever going to happen.'

'Are you sure.'

'Quite sure.'

'How can you know?'

Violet knew the answer to this one. 'If I said I didn't know, but I was still pretty sure, would that make you feel better?'

Shamira thought about this and sat up a bit straighter. 'My back hurts.'

'Do you want to get up?'

Violet stood up and held out her hands to help Shamira up. She took her hands and climbed to her feet.

Shamira blew air through her lips and shook her head, trying to shake off the past hour. 'I should start writing the next play, shouldn't I?'

Violet squeezed her arm warmly. 'I wasn't going to insist.'

Shamira dusted off her clothes and stood up. 'I really should. It's been months. I need to do something.'

Violet, still sitting on the floor looked up at her. 'What's it going to be about?'

Shamira scanned the room around her, taking in the old pots and pans and wilting plants sitting in the windowsill. 'A voyage to Mars.'

'Who is going to Mars?'

'Some lesbians.'

'Ah,' Violet said knowingly. 'And what happens on this voyage?'

'A great deal of interpersonal conflict.'

'Hmm. Is this based on anything in particular?'

'Not that I'm consciously aware of. Maybe you'd be able to pick up on inspirations I haven't thought of.'

'Provided you don't plagiarize again,' Violet joked.

Shamira shot her a deeply wounded look.

Violet's eyes glittered. 'Too soon?'

'Much too soon.'

Violet rubbed Shamira's upper back. 'I'm sorry.'

'Don't worry about it. I knew it was a joke. It was funny.'

'Good. I'm glad.'

'I'm laughing at it,' Shamira said, unsmiling.

'Yeah, I can tell.' Violet meant it. She knew Shamira was amused.

'But if you do think I'm getting too close to something you've seen before, you'll let me know?' Shamira asked.

Violet hummed thoughtfully. 'What if it's reminding me of something I've seen before but I'm almost certain you haven't?'

'Well, then that's a different situation, isn't it?'

'Do you want me to tell you if that ends up happening?' Violet considered getting up from sitting on the floor.

'I guess that depends upon how close it gets.'

'What if I'm completely certain it's something you've never seen before.'

'You're a great believer in coincidence, aren't you?'

'A very great believer. I think coincidence is much more common than almost anyone realises. I think there could be multiple bands of monkeys writing Romeo and Juliet on typewriters right now as we speak,' Violet said, intentionally obliterating her own point before she could even get to it.

'I think I want you to tell me if something even atmospherically or tonally reminds you of something else.' Shamira decided. 'If it ends up reminding you of the actual content of another work of fiction I would so much rather be safe than sorry.'

'What if something well and truly is coincidence, and then you just end up being sorry because you have decided not to pursue one of the best ideas you have ever had just because someone else has done something similar before?'

'You think the best ideas I could ever have could only be things other people have done before?'

'No! I didn't mean that!' Violet cried.

'That's what it sounds like. That's what seems to be happening to me.'

'That's not what's happening,' Violet insisted.

Shamira considered the question from a less reactive point of view. 'I think I would like to assess what risk I am in with regard to how my work is going to be perceived from as informed a point of view as possible. People on the internet are constantly accusing each other of plagiarism, even going so far as to claim that works which were written earlier were inspired by works that were written later, especially if the later work is more well-known or more controversial. I have read a lot of books, I have seen a lot of plays, I do not remember everything I have read or watched. There are, I'm sure, dozens of novels that you could tell me the titles of, and I would not be able to tell you whether or not I had read them.'

Violet laughed. 'I really don't feel like my memory is that much clearer or more powerful than yours.'

'Perhaps not, but you would be a second pair of eyes, and there are things you have seen that I have not seen. You would be able to predict what some people would think about a different set of ideas than the things that I would be able would be able to predict what they would react to.'

'Oh, that is a good point,' Violet nodded. 'I'm excited to read what you come up with.'

Shamira pulled a notebook off of a bookshelf and clicked the top of a pen a couple of times. 'Interior, spaceship. Am I allowed to start with "Interior, spaceship"?'

Violet stood up and stretched. 'Is it a screenplay? It reminds me of twenty other things, but if that's not a problem for you, then I would say, go for it.'

Shamira put pen to paper, and soon enough, words were flying. Evening fell and Violet opened the window to let in the outside air. It smelled of warm earth, strong-scented flowers, and decay. The city lights stained the clouds blue purple like a monochrome photograph.

Chapter Thirteen. Legal Drama

It was days later that Shamira appeared in court. The courtroom bore only a vague resemblance to what Richard had imagined a courtroom would look like. The wood was the wrong colour, it looked like pine rather than mahogany, and the windows were bigger. Richard had not expected there to be any windows at all. In his mind courtrooms were polished and steep and imposing and insurmountable. This room looked it was designed by someone who made dorm room furniture. There were curved lines and pops of brightly coloured paint or plastic. He felt like he could teach kindergarten in there and kids could store their bookbags under the counsel tables. It was difficult to feel worried in such a warm, generic space unless he imagined that he was there to take a test he had not studied for.

The trial was moving quickly. Richard and Shamira had the sense from the beginning of the day that the suit would be settled before the evening. They seemed to be out of luck. The plaintiff's attorneys were moving fast and there did not seem to be anything they could say to get them to slow down. Before Richard felt like he really had time to process what was happening, the judge announced that they were moving into closing arguments.

'According to subconscious doctrine, a defendant's motives or intentions are of no consequence to the question of infringement. Even if the defendant has no knowledge of the previous work's existence, damages may still be awarded. The sole criterion for plagiarism is the misappropriation of another's words as one's own without acknowledging the contribution or source,' the attorney at the stand reminded the room.

There was some murmuring of agreement.

'It applies to the use of ideas and expressions from another source as well. In this case we are dealing with rather more than that.'

It was true that passages of up to ten lines in *These Flowers Might Be Ours* matched scenes from *Roses and Thorns*.

'While Ralph Mawdsley noted in the fifth edition of Legal Problems of Religious and Private Schools that exact phrases may remain in a writer's consciousness long after even the knowledge that there was a prior source has been lost from memory, under the Copyright Act of 1976, subconscious copying is not a defense to action for damages.'

Richard tried to catch Shamira's eye from across the courtroom. No one cared about what she intended. They only seemed to care that the words on the page were the same. Shamira could not prove that she had never read *Roses and Thorns*. It had been established that she was part of a writer's group in the mid-2010s that Lilith Gibson, that work's playwright, had also participated in. Shamira's lawyer had tried to argue along the lines of coincidence, but she had been shut down by the argument that legal infringement of copyright had occurred regardless of how it had happened. If ten thousand monkeys with typewriters reproduced Stephen King's latest novel, they could also be sued for copyright infringement.

This seemed distinctly unfair to Richard—that one could break the law by accident with no way of being able to tell if your work was original and unique or just another wellspring bringing up water that had had already been drunk. It could be enough to scare someone away from writing anything at all. Richard could write and publish an article or a blog post tomorrow and someone could come along and say that he had stolen their way of phrasing something and there would not be any way for him to prove that he had not. The law had no way of distinguishing between memory and independent creation.

'Copyright protects the content of a literary work without regard for intent to plagiarize.' The attorney continued. 'If, the defendant's claim of coincidental patterns in storytelling and subconscious recall of dialogue are the verifiable and substantiable truth, it does not alter the fact that the text of her play constitutes reproduction of a substantial part of Lilith Gibson's *Roses and Thorns*. This reproduction constitutes probative similarity beyond what could reasonably be considered coincidental. As discussed earlier, we have shown that the defendant had reasonable access to Miss Gibson's manuscript. We therefore may presume copying-in-fact. As the West End production of Miss Shamira Allis's play has generated substantial income—'

'Not for me, it hasn't,' Shamira muttered under her breath.

'This will mandate the closure of the production.'

There was a collective sigh from the defense.

'And award damages of twenty thousand dollars to Miss Gibson.'

Richard felt the reality of what he had gotten Shamira into hit him all at once. Tens of thousands of pounds of debt on top of legal fees, all because he had believed she could defend her honor and her artistry in a court of law. There was never going to be a future for *These Flowers Might Be Ours*, not after the day the letter from America landed on their south London doorstep. Richard had clung to an ideal of truth and justice in the face of reason and reality. Shamira had listened to him for no other reason than that she loved him. She had trusted his judgment in defiance against her own instincts and he had led her astray. All of the trouble they were in now was his own fault and it would be up to him to make it right. He owed that to Shamira.

Shamira looked over at him from across the court room, her face blank, a mask of stunned defeat. Then her lips twitched into a half-smile and Richard felt the weight of tears in his throat. She held nothing against him. This was never going to change anything between them.

Rising panic began to creep over Richard, a swift incoming tide swallowing up swathes of dry land. A lot could go very wrong very quickly and even the biggest mistakes of his life were not going to make anyone stop listening to him. They were in hot water now. He just hoped he would be able to think of a way out without making anything worse.

In a digital audio workstation open on her laptop computer, Kiran was working on a solo project. She had been trying to keep it on the back burner while they were on tour, but ideas kept bubbling to the surface. She carried a notebook of paper ruled with musical staves and had a sketchbook with her at all times. Kiran had been writing down several different versions of the songs she had been working on.

She answered the phone and listened for a few seconds before responding. 'Oh yeah, I stole both of those riffs. You can go ahead and use them in whatever you want.'

Unperturbed, Kiran smiled and returned to adjusting track levels.

Morgan Garrett had told Shamira before the time they were appointed to meet in the café that they would be wearing a blue jumper and a backpack. The account they had used to message Shamira had been private and they had not responded to Shamira's follow request. They had also evidently deleted their official public account from their time as a Member of Parliament. It occurred to Shamira that she might be meeting a murderer. At least she knew she would have her colleagues to back her up. Except for Cathryn. Cathryn would be out the backdoor before Shamira knew what was happening. She scanned the steady stream of people walking past the shop for someone in blue with a backpack.

What she was not expecting to see was the lawyer who had read out the closing argument landing her in tens of thousands of dollars of debt the day before pushing open the door and walking up to her.

Shamira turned around as though in slow-motion. Her ceramic coffee cup slipped from her fingers and dropped to the floor, shattering on impact. Scalding black coffee splashed onto her trouser legs.

Morgan, for it was they, gaped at her, mouth falling open and then seemed to catch themself. 'I'm so sorry,' they gasped.

Shamira looked down at the shattered coffee cup, noticing it for the first time. 'Don't worry about it.'

They both reached for the mental box dispensing tissue at the same time.

'Sorry, sorry,' Shamira said.

'Let me— Did you get burned?' Morgan had managed to get a handful of tissues before Shamira did, and awkwardly handed them to her.

'Not really, I just— My hand slipped—'

'I didn't mean to startle you. I thought you would have recognized my name.'

Shamira worried then that she might be looking foolish. She recalled the name Garrett from the trial, but she should have recognized their face from television. It made sense, didn't it? Morgan was a politician. Loads of politicians practiced law before going into politics.

Morgan considered asking if there was a broom that they could use to sweep up the broken ceramic. There didn't seem to be one behind the bar. 'I hope you're not in too much difficulty as a result of the decision. I'm afraid you didn't have much of a chance going in.'

'I had a sense of that, but I was persuaded otherwise.'

'You should seek better counsel next time.'

'You're telling me.'

Morgan stepped gingerly around the broken pieces of the coffee cup and the spreading pool on the floor. They reached one of the tall chairs facing the street, turned the chair so it was facing Shamira and sat down. 'You wanted to know about Robert Douglas?'

'You auditioned for him?'

'Someone had dropped out of the production. I think he wanted to work on *Roses and Thorns* because it was about a high school swim team.'

'Holy shit,' Shamira gasped, realising what Morgan was implying.

'It gets worse. He wanted me to sign a non-disclosure agreement right there in the audition room, apparently thinking I would not read it.'

'Did he have any idea of who you were?'

'Did you?' Morgan asked.

'Good point.'

'And then, when I refused, he told me something about how I was disrespectful and would never work in this town again.'

Shamira let out a long breath. 'That's a bit more than weird vibes.'

'He seemed really out of it, so I wasn't sure what to make of the situation. I did get the sense that the previous person had pulled out due to some abuse. I don't know the specifics; you would have to figure out who they were.'

It was dawning on Shamira just how serious of a situation this was. 'Do you have any idea why no one else reached out? Do you think there were other NDAs? Would you know how to help them speak out?'

'I could probably do something if I knew who they were.'

'I don't quite understand why no one would have come forward. Even if there were agreements or they were afraid, wouldn't at least one person take the risk to try to make sure no one else was putting themselves in danger?'

'You know that's not how it goes.'

Shamira sat down beside Morgan. They were right. There was the whole history of the entertainment industry to show for it. She closed her eyes in exhaustion. 'What do you think he did?'

Morgan shook their head. 'Could be anything. I don't think there's anything I would put past him.'

'At least he's dead,' Shamira said, momentarily forgetting that this was not general knowledge.

'Robert Douglas is dead?' Morgan sat up a bit straighter and then, slowly, began to smile.

'He died at the beginning of the month.'

Morgan frowned. 'How do you actually know Robert Douglas?'

'My partner was one of the people who found the body.'

'What?' this was not what Morgan had expected when they had agreed to meet Shamira Allis at a coffee shop.

'It was in a car park.'

'A car park? Where?'

'A few blocks from here.'

'How did you find out he was directing something?'

'His brother had some of his papers and if you sifted enough his name was associated with some casting calls. Not easy to trace at all.'

'How did he die? He was young.'

'We're not sure,' Shamira admitted.

'Hang on. Oxford Circus car park? This wouldn't be the same person that Layne Thompson paid for the funeral of?'

'You read about that?'

Morgan looked defeated. 'I'd fallen asleep in Parliament. I wanted some insight into how other people dealt with unexpected.'

'So, we wanted to figure out what was happening with him before that.'

Clouds were gathering high in the sky and one passed over the sun, shading and softening everything. 'It wasn't being considered as a murder,' Morgan said quietly.

Shamira let out a breathy little laugh. 'Who said anything about murder?'

'I was just thinking that if he did even half of the things that I'm fearing he did, I would not necessarily blame anyone,' Morgan said gravely.

'Did you try any criminal cases when you were a lawyer?'

'No, it was strictly litigation.'

'If you did, would you want to be persecution or defense?' Shamira was trying to gauge where Morgan stood.

'I want to do some good in the world. If someone were in danger of being unjustly sentenced I would want to be the persecution. Persecution decides the sentences. It's all about subterfuge and infiltration. That's what people say, people really trying to figure out what they can do. They say if you can stomach it, if you can handle putting yourself in that position, become a lawyer for the persecution.'

Shamira blinked slowly. 'Morgan Garrett, how much money do you think I have?'

'I know how much money you have.'

'I can't afford to pay the damages or even really the legal fees.'

'Then you're going to have to find someone who can help you. You profited from someone else's work. I don't know what to tell you.'

'Don't you have any pity?' Shamira asked, almost coolly.

'I have a great deal of pity, I'm afraid it has not been very helpful to me.'

'I didn't want to go forward with challenging the lawsuit.'

'You did not intend to plagiarize either, but that hardly serves to alter the outcome of your actions.'

'Is this meant to be about teaching me a lesson?'

Morgan considered this. The spilled coffee on the floor had stopped spreading out now and had settled into a sticky puddle. It would probably take some scrubbing to get it up off the wood. 'No. I don't think so.'

'You've put me in this position.'

'I really haven't. There wasn't anything I could do.'

Shamira sniffed. 'The road to hell is paved with "there wasn't anything I could do".'

'That's certainly true, but I feel like you're going to be able to work something out.'

'I hope you're right.'

'So, Robert Douglas may have been killed in a West End car park?' Morgan observed.

'You said it, not me.'

'What if we can't get in contact with any of the people that he worked with?'

'Well, if he's dead then he won't be bothering them anymore, will he?'

'I suppose you're right.' It occurred to Shamira that Morgan may have known much more than they were letting on. But she might have been wrong and if she wasn't, how would she be able to get them to say any more than they had already said? 'Do you think it would be for the best to just let sleeping dogs lie, so to speak?'

'That depends upon what lies they're telling,' Morgan replied.

'What do you mean by that?'

Morgan laughed, mostly out of awkwardness. 'I was making a joke, you know, sit, stay, speak, let sleeping dogs lie?'

Shamira was lost. 'If you say so.'

'But I agree. It's probably best to allow the unexplained death of Robert Douglas to remain unexplained.'

Shamira nodded, moving some of the broken ceramic under the counter with the side of her shoe. 'It may be best. At least I feel like I'm walking away from this conversation with more information than I started with.'

'I'm glad I could be of some help,' Morgan said, getting up to leave.

'Wait, before you go could I make you a coffee or something?'

This momentarily baffled Morgan, but Shamira had dropped a cup on the floor and not seemed too worried about it, so perhaps they should have guessed earlier. 'Do you work here?' Morgan asked.

'Yeah,' Shamira admitted.

'Why didn't you say so?'

Shamira put up her hands in surrender. 'You suggested the place. I didn't want to make it awkward.'

'I didn't know how long we would be here, it's the only place in the area that's open late.'

'Well, um, obviously I'm not on the clock, but did you want anything?' she offered again.

'It's a bit late for coffee.'

'I guess you're right. Thank you for your help.'

'I'm sorry I couldn't do more.'

'No, you're not.' Shamira wasn't sure why she felt so comfortable around Morgan that she could speak to them this directly without fear of being misinterpreted. Normally, she would be petrified that her usual, much less snarky repartee would be misinterpreted but somehow she got the sense that there was very little she could do to get on Morgan's bad side. It was strange but the day before she could have sworn she was on the wrong side of the lawyer named Garrett and certain that they would give her no quarter no matter what she did. But here she was, watching disgraced politician Morgan Garrett putting their backpack back on and offering to get them coffee. It was odd what a bit of hypothetical letting off of hypothetical vigilante action could do.

Morgan left the café through the front door, letting the latch close softly behind them, and Shamira turned her attention to the mess she had made. She was almost certain she was imagining it but down on the floor where the puddle of coffee met some minor seepage from a nearly empty bin underneath the ledge table looking out on the street, she could have sworn she saw tiny fizzing bubbles. In the very bottom of the bin there was nothing but a few scraps of dried-out salad leaves from long ago. If Shamira's undergraduate roommate's refrigerator misadventures were anything to go by they were three or four weeks old. They had clearly escaped from the bin liner after someone had scraped their plate into the bin long ago.

The café brewed coffee with neutral pH water rather than the lime-y Thames tap water, a decision Shamira had never understood as it was widely known that coffee tasted richer brewed with alkaline water. But why was there fizzing? Green leaf lettuce typically had an acidic pH around the same as that of coffee brewed with water that was neither hard nor soft. Shamira had figured this out experimenting with smoothies—lettuce and milk tasted less horrible together than one might imagine.

She filed these observations away, not sure who ask about what they might mean, and went to go find some rags to clean up the coffee and a brush to sweep up the broken ceramic.

On the bus on the way back home Shamira texted Violet, asking for the phone number of that teenager Layne had evidently decided was in charge of the murder investigation and the drummer who seemed to know everything about plants. She wanted to find out what could have caused the unexpected chemical reaction underneath the bin in the café and she had a feeling they might have an idea of what could have caused it.

Chapter Fourteen. Destroy The Evidence

Layne had used Autumn's practice's online booking service to get in contact with her. Autumn was moderately annoyed by this because Layne had Autumn's personal phone number and Autumn had tried, repeatedly, to get Layne removed from their list of clients. Despite Autumn's best efforts, including contriving to not be in at the hour that Layne said they were coming by, an attempt at doorbell chicken and reaching through the letter slot to hang a do-not-disturb sign on the doorknob, Layne was once again lounging on the worn-out couch and Autumn was once again perched on the exceedingly hard chair.

Layne threw an arm over their face like an actor in a silent film. Autumn watched them silently, implacably.

Layne did not drop any of the drama, but eventually dropped their arm and said 'It's not working. None of it is working.'

Autumn picked up the tin of biscuits she had bought for the coffee table and attempted to pry the lid off of it. It did not budge but she diligently persisted in making an elaborate show of devoting all of their attention to trying to remove the circle of molded metal.

'I've been trying to get myself accused of murder.'

Autumn flipped over the biscuit tin to see if she could get more leverage that way. She tapped around the edge of the tin to see if she could hear if there was something inside jamming it closed. After a minute or so she acknowledged Layne with a disinterested 'Uh-huh.'

'It hasn't been working. People either seem to think that I'm not capable of it or that I'm beyond reproach. Everyone who thinks I have the nerve thinks I'm too principled and everyone who thinks I'd do it thinks I haven't got the guts. It's getting quite annoying.'

This was almost interesting enough to get Autumn to stop wrestling with the biscuit tin, but she had managed to get the lid to shift a couple of millimeters and she was considering trying to slide something between the lid and the rest of the box. Perhaps something like the edge of the flap of the envelope containing Layne's file. 'And how is that going for you?' she asked, as though Layne had just told them they had started working as a dog walker.

Layne stretched out on the couch so that they were almost laying out full-length. 'It's going absolutely nowhere. There have been no suspicions directed toward me.'

The lid of the tin slipped just a little bit more and Autumn actually took in what she had just heard. 'Wait. Was I one of the people you were trying to pique the suspicions of?'

Layne shifted on the couch, trying to get comfortable. 'Obviously.'

After a few more taps and tugs, Autumn set down the tin. 'You wanted me to suspect that you personally had murdered Robert Douglas?'

'No,' Layne rolled her eyes. 'I wanted you to suspect that I had impersonally murdered him.'

'What did you think I was going to do about this?'

'I don't know, apply all of your famous expertise to confirming or denying your suspicions?'

Autumn sat forward on her chair. 'Now hang on, I would only confirm or deny my suspicions based on actual verifiable evidence. I would not make a decision or form a final opinion unless I actually knew whether or not you had done it. I do actually know what I'm doing.'

'That's what you keep saying,' Layne sighed. 'You've been saying that like you've already made up your mind. Like you think it's impossible that I could have killed him, just like everybody else.'

Autumn almost wished she had not put down the biscuit tin. 'You do know whether or not you did it, don't you?' she laughed nervously.

'Oh, I'm crystal clear on what I have and have not done.'

'Good,' Autumn said skeptically. 'Because that has not always been the case.'

'I just wish someone would suspect me. They knew I was in the area. I'm sick of being seen as some kind of unimpeachable innocent.'

'Well, it would be a lot more difficult to accuse you than some other people. You do have a pretty unimpeachable track record,' Autumn offered, trying to crack the surface to get at what was happening beneath it.

'No, I don't,' Layne said, almost whining. Then they sat up, mustering their internal forces and repeated in a harsh whisper 'No, I don't.'

Slowly, as though with vast long-suffering resignation, Autumn took out a notebook and a pen. She clicked the pen once. 'Is there something you're trying to get punished for? Something you've done that you're seeking absolution for?'

Layne shook their head. 'Not in those terms.'

'So, is it actually attention that you're after?' Autumn asked. They might be heading back into familiar territory.

'No,' Layne said firmly. 'That's not what this is about.'

'You couldn't be much more in the public eye than you are now,' Autumn was frightened of the possibilities of what Autumn could be getting at, but she tried not to show it.

Layne shrugged languidly. 'I could be above the fold.'

Autumn's pen hovered above the page. 'Do you actually want to be a headline?'

Layne laughed, a derisive little giggle. 'No, I'm just being pedantic.'

Autumn made a note, worry written on her face more clearly than it was on the page. 'What is this about then? Or do you not want to tell me?'

Layne swallowed another giggle. 'No, you're right. There is something that I did. Something I am ashamed of. It was years and years ago. I don't think it would make any difference if it was brought to light now.'

'Then why not actually say what it was? Why not clear the air?'

Layne squirmed on the couch. 'It's something very bad. Something that I would change if I could only change one thing about how I have lived my life. What's really wearing down on me is that it's hypocritical. I know what I would do to someone if I found out that they had done what I had done to someone.'

'If I promise not to tell, would you tell me what you have done?'

'I'm not convinced I can take you at your word. I'm not sure that I can trust you anymore,' Layne said.

'Because I told Ash what you were trying to do?' Autumn asked.

'You betrayed client confidentiality,' Layne accused.

'You weren't my client anymore and it was in the service of the investigation. Ash would have gone down the wrong path if they had started following the red herrings you had left for them.'

'What did you think I was trying to do? Did you think that I didn't have fail safes?' there was a disturbed laughter bubbling beneath Layne's words. 'That I hadn't worked everything out so that nothing would go wrong?'

'I think I have some sense of what you were trying to do, but you'll have to forgive me if I don't share your certainty in what the outcomes of your actions are going to be.'

'I want to make things difficult for myself because I feel guilty. There. I said it. Does that make you feel better?'

'No,' Autumn frowned deeply. 'Does it make you feel better? Is it something you wanted to get off your chest?'

Layne considered this and let out a long breath. They weren't sure. Then all the emotion and turmoil they had simultaneously been holding in and attempting to excavate and drag out into the open came crashing through. They sobbed, a hiccupping, unexpectedly quavering sound.   'Sometimes I feel like there are hundreds of people sitting in judgment over my every action.'

Autumn looked at Layne with tulle-veiled pity. 'People have their own problems, why would they be so overwhelmingly preoccupied with yours?'

'Because they have been in the past.' Layne took in quick breaths and spoke rapidly as though if they did not speak now, they would lose their chance to forever. 'It's probably categorically paranoia but I know the way that I am feeling is influenced by things that have happened in the past that I was not aware of at the time that I only found out about years later. Tell me that's not enough to make anyone wary and over-cautious?'

'You don't seem to be behaving in a way that is over-cautious. Or cautious at all, actually.'

Something seemed to brush aside Layne's nervousness with all the finality of a street-sweeper on a Monday morning. They sat up in a single fluid motion and sat primly as though they had not been sprawled out across the entire sofa. 'Not anymore. I used to be cautious. Now I have thrown caution to the wind.'

'How are you feeling about this?' Autumn took Layne's cue indicating a return to a semblance of normalcy.

'You're not my therapist.'

'No, I'm not, I'm your friend."

'I ruined someone's career. That's what I'm feeling guilty about. It was ages and ages ago and I dragged their name through the mud. A lot of people were upset with how a screenwriter I knew nearly a decade ago wrote a gay couple and I precipitated a pile-on of denouncement that I think ruined him. It was almost accidental, but I know I acted with malice in my heart.'

Autumn attempted to pick her way through this. 'I don't think you can have single-handedly ended someone's career, especially before—if you don't mind me saying—before you really had one of your own. I don't think the court of public opinion works like that. People can have their careers unaffected by outright bigotry and committing actual atrocities, I hardly think that the opinion of one young person—'

Layne was shaking their head rapidly. 'You don't understand.'

'You're right, I don't.'

'I can be very influential when I want to be. I'm actually very good at manipulating people when I'm careful not to make any mistakes. I can lay a web of circumstances that people stumble into. It's not something I'm proud of but it's an ability I've been aware of since childhood. I've generally tried to avoid acting on my impulses to lay out circumstances like that. I know that when I did before I ended up ruining someone. It was not my intention but what I did was by no means simple.'

Autumn's pen flew across the page. She pressed her lips together and exhaled through her nose. 'Is this why you are so upset that no one has accused you of murder? Because you've arranged the circumstances to make yourself appear suspicions. In a way pulling the opposite trick of what you tried with that author—'

'Screenwriter.' Layne corrected.

'Right, screenwriter—all those years ago?' Autumn asked.

'Something like that,' Layne said glumly.

'Well, if it is something like that, I would think that might prove that what happened to the screenwriter was not as much your fault as it may have seemed like it was.'

'No,' Layne said, and there was a hollowness and finality to the syllable that chilled Autumn's blood.

Autumn nodded. 'Alright.'

'It's something like that, but it isn't that. If I were to actually enact a version of what I did then I would have been in prison weeks ago. I wanted to know what would happen if I only put myself in suspicion's way but did not force anything.'

'And you've been disappointed with the result?' Autumn confirmed.

'Not with the circumstantial result,' Layne clarified. 'More like disappointed by how some people have reacted.'

'Do you think this is connected with your previous attempts to manipulate the opinions of others?' Autumn asked.

'I think I've just been thinking about it again lately and it's made me feel guilty.'

'That's understandable. Is there anything you could do now to try to alleviate the effects of what you did to that writer?'

'I could issue some kind of statement explaining my current point of view,' Layne considered.

'And what is that current point of view?' Autumn inquired.

'That he's a poorly-informed bastard that should be more mindful of the effect of his work on an audience but that he's not as big of an asshole as a lot of people thought,' Layne answered honestly.

'Would that—' Autumn tried to fight a smile, 'Would that be helpful to you?'

Layne squinted at the biscuit tin on the table. 'Did you crush all the biscuits in there when you were tugging and banging on the lid?'

Autumn looked at Layne as though they had missed an entire lecture pointedly directed at them. 'There aren't biscuits in there. I opened it and took them out and put all of the biscuits in Tupperware when I first bought the tin. They're in the kitchen if you want one. It's full of pincushions and measuring tapes. That's why it won't open.'

'That doesn't seem very useful,' Layne observed.

'It's not about being useful,' Autumn sniffed.

'I would have thought that people put sewing supplies in biscuit tins because it was convenient, because they were sturdy and the right size,' Layne argued.

'Maybe so,' Autumn said, striking the lid of the tin so it closed firmly once again. This made a loud sound and Layne jumped a little.

'Sorry about that,' Autumn said, not meaning it.

'Don't worry about it,' Layne said, with warm insincerity.

'You know, for someone who is allegedly not having a crisis, you seem to be very good at panicking,' Autumn said.

'Thanks a lot,' Layne laughed.

'Any time.'

Chapter Fifteen. Handbook For Despair

'Saving Atlantiades,' was the name of Ash's favorite song by The Stone Dandelions. It was an anthem claimed by nonbinary and intersex fans although there was some pushback against this reading by people who claimed that it was specifically about male survivorship of sexual assault. It was based on the Ancient Greek story of Hermaphroditus and Salamis. The song title was a play on the book Saving Ophelia incorporating one of the Greek names of Hermaphroditus. It was essentially sad indie pop, although there was a lot of distortion on the guitars.

It told the story of a young person who had discovered who they were only to be pursued by someone who was trying to change them to make them fit better into a boy-meets-girl love story. They run away from their pursuant and just before the moment of their capture the narrator intervenes, freezing the image and asking if there was any way out, if there was anyone else who could save them and, if not, how could they save themselves, what were their options. At the bridge of the song the moment of suspended animation ends, and you hear Atlantiades' thoughts the moment before they are chased into the water. It was utterly heartrending and profoundly, resolutely hopeful, and fiercely defiant. When Ash found themself in need of fortification or resolve or healing, they would frequently put it on and crank the volume up. It always made them feel like there was a way out or a way to make things better even if they had not yet figured out what it was.

They put it on now, standing in their dimly lit kitchen wondering what to do next, where to turn, because they had figured it out.

They had not necessarily expected to have figured out what had happened so quickly but now they felt more trapped than they could ever recall feeling in their life. They knew they were not going to go to the authorities with what they had discovered but they did not know whether or not they should tell anyone at all what they had realised. The trouble was if they kept the truth to themself people would realise they were concealing something. Ash was generally a good liar because they never had to worry about forgetting the details of their falsehood. Indeed, when they kept up a lie for a long time they often half-convinced themselves that it was true, carrying around two versions of the past, neither more real than the other, one simply more convenient.

But Ash could not come up with a version of events where they had not figured out how Robert Douglas had died. They also could not come up with a different solution that would explain all the facts and result in less, rather than more, trouble and strife. They could not come up with a way out it. They had revealed their true colours too early, they had shown their hand and now there could be no bluffing. What were their options? They could run away. That might prove temporarily moderately successful, but it was embarrassing, and they were sure it would reveal exactly what they knew no less clear than if they went out and shouted it through a megaphone on the street corner. They could claim that they were no longer interested in trying to solve the mystery. That would be seen as cowardice and only show that they did not trust Layne and Violet. It was by far the safest option, but they did not think they were going to take it.

Layne would definitely realise that Ash had pieced together exactly what had happened and there was a chance that Violet might as well. They could gather everyone together and say exactly what they had discovered, scene by scene and moment by moment like they were the detective in an Agatha Christie novel. That was the most dangerous option. For one thing they would be in the same room as a murderer who knew they knew they were a murderer. That option would take the most trust, the most belief that the people they had been working with the past couple of weeks—the subject of their celebrity hyper-fixation, they reminded themself—would have their back.

They listened to the words of the song, trying, perhaps foolishly, to forget how intricately the voice singing the words was bound up in the whole affair. Layne Thompson wasn't singing to give you better perspective on the potential dangers of Layne Thompson, they were not trying to give you comfort for how you felt about them and the fact that they may not be the person you hoped they were. Or were they?

On the recording Layne came in for the last verse up the octave.

I don't know what to say to help

But you might if you listen
Wind through the willows, reeds and kelp
Hope aches more than despair
So, you hold on and on and on
To what they can't ensnare

Ash decided to follow their instincts. They had yet to be led astray following what they deeply felt would be the best course of action. They were going get an explanation scene. They were going show everyone how it was done.

***

On the last day of his life, Robert Douglas had a late lunch in a small, busy café in Covent Garden. It was on the corner of a block with large south-facing windows looking out onto a zebra crossing that constantly poured with people crossing the street.

He ordered a salad and a coffee, told the girl behind the counter to hurry up, he did not have all day, what was she standing around gawping like that for, and looked grumpily out the window. The table was not clean. It was covered in flakes of pastry crumbs and stained rings left by coffee and milk. Douglas looked down at it with distaste but there was no other table open in the café.

'Can someone get over here and clean this? It's disgusting?' he said loudly. The girl and boy behind the counter looked at each other as though they were deciding on whether or not ignore his request. 'This is why people say our generation is entitled,' he said, staring them down.

The girl behind the counter giggled. She shook her head. 'It really is.'

'Then why don't you get over here and clean it?' Robert stood up so she could reach the table to clean it once she came over there.

'I'm very sorry, we're understaffed.'

'I'm very sorry, sir,' Robert corrected.

'What was that?' the girl asked. Infuriatingly she seemed to be fighting a smile.

'I said "I'm very sorry, *sir*,"' Robert repeated through gritted teeth. He was really getting annoyed now.

'Oh, that's alright. I accept your apology. Your food will be ready in a minute.'

Robert Douglas was so baffled and angry that he had to sit down to process what had just happened.

The girl brought his mushroom salad to his table, setting the ceramic plate on top of the coffee rings and handed him a fork and knife wrapped in tissue. He took it from her hand and for a moment their hands touched.

'I'm getting a divorce, you know,' he said.

The girl quickly withdrew her hand and took a step back. 'That's nice,' she said.

'No. It's not nice, it's divorce.'

She had already retreated behind the counter. Robert looked down at his salad grimly, but his mood was lifted by the beautiful plate before him. It did not look like a salad from a place where tables were covered in sticky rings of coffee and syrup and milk. It looked like plates he had seen in Michelin starred restaurants. There was absolutely nothing disappointing about it. He briefly attempted to be annoyed that there were no elements of the salad that he could find fault with but the crisp smell of the freshly washed and spun leaves, perfectly fresh, broke his resolve.

The salad had Caesar's mushrooms and several different kinds of lettuce. It was arranged delicately on the plate with dressing drizzled in a spiral. The fork and knife that had been wrapped in the tissue were still warm from the dishwasher. His coffee hadn't shown up yet.

He took a forkful of the salad. It was perfectly dressed, and the mushrooms were some of the best that he had ever tasted. He tried to hold on to how aggravated he was, but instead he was focused on the meal. He was almost emotionally moved. The flavor reminded him of some deep, indistinct sense of nostalgia—of memories he was not previously aware of rising to the surface.

The sun shifted, bouncing off the glass façade of the office building across the street. It was shining at a low angle, sharp and piercing. It gradually began to sting his eyes, like he had rubbed his eyes after handling chili oil. He brought the tissue that had been wrapped around the distastefully warm flatware and wiped at the corners of his eyes. This did not seem to help very much. He turned his head to try to see if there were any open tables in cooler, darker regions of the café.

Looking too directly into the reflected sunlight had evidently done something to his vision as the café swam in indistinct shapes and fields of colour. The world seemed to have gone soft and mutable, like if he looked away and looked back what he was seeing would shift before his eyes. A thudding pain arrived behind his eyes. He clambered to his feet and stumbled towards the door, stepping out into the street. The sun was still in his eyes so he could not see much. He thought he heard shouting behind him. As though guided by instinct he crossed at the zebra crossing to the shadier side of the street.

There was a pain in his stomach building to a nausea and he felt his heartrate speed up. What had happened? Robert Douglas did not consider himself easily disturbed, but this was a thoroughly inaccurate opinion he held of himself. Robert Douglas was very easily disturbed. He moved through the world in a near constant state of disgruntlement, taking issue with almost every facet of daily life he stumbled across. He would, however, never in a million years consider this being sensitive. Had something frightened him? Had the disrespect of the girl in the coffee shop been so disagreeable that his body was physically reacting to it? The pain was growing in intensity but he did not feel that he could vomit or that that would help. He continued down the street as though he could somehow outrun the pain. It made an odd kind of sense. If he kept moving he would not stay in one place or one moment long enough to realise how bad it was. He wasn't paying much attention to where he was going, and he could not really see very well either. The world was still swimming. He stumbled on, trying to stay in the shade as best as he could tell where the shade was falling from the sporadically planted trees. There came a moment where he felt like the pain was leveling off and he might be able to think more clearly. He decided he could start walking some of the way home and when he got there he could take some painkillers and try to sleep off whatever was happening. With this thought in mind, he headed north, only a little unsteadily.

One block later, there came a wave of blinding pain more severe than anything he had ever experienced before. He tried to think of what he could compare it to but even trying to think that thought was drowned out by the intensity of the pain. His heart was beating as fast as it would be if he were sprinting as fast as he could.

He felt suddenly as though he was about to collapse and reached out, managing to grab the wrought iron fence outside of someone's house. The wave of pain passed, and he thought about how incredible it was that he did not cry out. He felt quite certain that anyone else would be screaming. Anyone less iron-willed than Robert Douglas would be screaming in agony. Feeling quite smug and assured by this he continued walking. He was sure that everything was going to be alright.

Passing a car park he decided he could make better time by cutting across the car park only halfway across he decided that there was no harm in sitting down and taking a little break leaning against someone's car. He was feeling quite uncomfortable. After he took a moment he could keep going and walk the rest of the way home.

He felt a pain in his chest and collapsed from sitting to lying on the pavement. That was the last moment Robert Douglas was consciously aware of experiencing.

Chapter Sixteen. The Airspeed Velocity of a Dove In Freefall

They met in the hotel. Ash would have preferred to have met in their apartment. It would have given them more control over the space but there was always the danger of their parents demanding to know what was going on and they might decide that more people had to know the details of Robert Douglas's death than was truly necessary. They asked Richard, Layne, Shamira, Kiran, Mila, Morgan and Autumn to meet them in the seventh-story suite at six in the evening. They had gathered all the chairs from the bandmember's rooms and arranged them in a circle with the sofas that were already in the room. It did not have quite the energy of the final scene of the screen adaptation of a Christie novel, but there was a quiet menacing sense of drama that they quite liked, the kind that only issues from the uncanny of large hotels built in the late twentieth century. Once everyone was settled with cups of tea or coffee or something they had taken from the minibar on The Stone Dandelion's budget, Ash looked around and stood up.

All attention was on them. They cleared their throat. 'You have probably guessed why I have gathered you here today.'

'Have you always wanted to say that?' Autumn asked, somewhat giddily.

'I have determined the sequence of events leading to the death of one Mr. Robert Douglas in the Oxford Circus car park at half six in the afternoon on Saturday the second of July.' Ash began. 'I have accomplished this by determining the facts through a number of channels and making several key inferences.'

'It went like this—' Ash glanced at Layne, for confirmation to continue, for confirmation that they would add in the pieces Ash was missing. It was a mad story. If Layne denied it they would look completely reasonable. 'The cast and crew of the Camden Fringe production of Lilith Gibson's play *Roses and Thorns* wrote a piece of fan mail to The Stone Dandelions, ostensibly to let them know that they would be using covers of some of their songs in the production—'

'"Saving Atlantiades" and "Cold, Dark, Earth,"' Layne specified, showing nothing but enthusiasm for the band's songs.

'Those were the ones. But they also coded a message into the letter. It was a cry for help. It was a relatively simple hidden message using spelling errors. I discovered this letter in a desk drawer shortly before you all arrived. The coded message said "THREAT TO LIFE KILL THE DIRECTOR."'

There wasn't much of an audible reaction in the room. More of a hushed murmur and a leaning in to hear what Ash would say next.

'I can see this does not surprise many of you,' Ash said, looking around. 'It did not surprise me either. I was not sure that I would find such a message, but I had my suspicions that one had been received. This letter was read, I believe, by all members of the band. The coded message, was however, I believe, deciphered by only one.'

Everyone in the circle looked around at each other.

'Yesterday evening, Ms. Shamira Allis discovered a curious chemical reaction between strong-brewed acidic coffee and seepage from vegetative matter below a bin in a coffee shop in the West End. Ms. Mila Becard explained to me last night that there is a type of alkaloid that only occurs in plants. These Pyrrolizidine alkaloids are toxins occurring in thousands of plant species, including high concentrations in nightshade and oleander. However, to achieve the type of reaction that Ms. Allis reports observing, there would likely have to be a higher concentration still than naturally occurs. Ms. Becard and I obtained a sample of the matter adhered to the inside of the bin in the café and visual taxonomic categorization confirmed that it was, indeed deadly nightshade and chemical testing indicated that additional alkaloid toxins had been sprinkled on the leaves. To me this indicates that our killer had a flare for the poetic, belladonna is, after all, the songwriter's poison, but also that they did not want to leave anything up to chance. They did not leave Mr. Douglas enough time to seek out an antidote or other medical assistance. Mixed in with the desiccated nightshade leaves were traces of green leaf lettuce and Cesar's mushrooms. I found the mushrooms particularly curious because Cesar's mushrooms are famously difficult to distinguish from death cap mushrooms. Was this a failed attempt at adding more poison to the pile, another verse of poetry, or simply a component of the salad that sealed the fate of Robert

Douglas. I'm not sure I can tell you, but I have a pretty good idea of who could.'

There were several intakes of breath. Ash waited. Nobody said anything. Ash continued.

'Someone in this room wanted to do right by a group of people they had not met before they wrote to them asking for their help. Someone had spent too long feeling disturbed by and ill-at-ease with death. Most murders occur in the heat of the moment. Most violent deaths are crimes of passion. This was no such murder. The death of Robert Douglas was planned and executed with the intent to preserve the lives, livelihood and wellbeing of the cast and crew of the play *Roses and Thorns*. Ironically, or because the universe has an odd sense of humor, this is the very same play that successfully sued Ms. Shamira Allis for copyright infringement. Morgan Garrett, an attorney on that case has confirmed the nature of the threats to the cast and crew on the production.'

Mila raised her hand and Ash stopped speaking. 'I was wondering if Garrett was able to confirm who the cast members of that production actually were?' Mila inquired.

Everyone turned to Morgan. 'I have received some correspondence from them but they have asked that their identities by kept secret,' Morgan said.

'But you actually do know who they are?' Mila persisted.

'You said you would be able to help them if you knew who they were,' Shamira remembered.

'I did say that.' Morgan agreed. 'What I did not say was that I would let any of the rest of you know if I did.'

'You told me that you didn't know who they were,' Shamira said, trying to conceal a note of betrayal.

Ash could see that they were losing the room. 'This individual may have been provided with some proof or evidence of Douglas's behavior. Or they may have simply taken their correspondents at their word. I do not believe that this letter—" Here Ash placed the letter in question on the hotel desk under the mirror on the wall, "constitutes the sole communication between the cast of *Roses and Thorns* and the member of The Stone Dandelions who elected to answer their call. I believe there was some collaboration on the nature of the plan and when it would be carried out. However, I have no evidence of this. This person would have to have had at least a passing familiarity with plant toxins and their pathology. Ms. Mila Becard is known to write a blog focusing on mycology.'

There was a shift as everyone seemed to re-evaluate the questions that Mila had just asked Morgan. Ash waited, but once again, no one said anything.

'I believe this blog is evidence that Mila was not the poisoner. Mila Becard has written extensively on the toxicology of organic poisons. I believe that if Mila wanted to poison someone it would be nearly untraceable—'

'I'd be able to figure it out,' Kiran asserted. 'She's predictably unpredictable.'

'Thank you, Kiran,' Ash said, not knowing how else to respond. 'The poisoning that occurred was haphazard, I believe deliberately so. A full autopsy was never performed on the body of Robert Douglas. One person was lied to about whether or not an autopsy was carried out. This was because they had made repeated requests to be present during the procedure. I do not know whether they were aware prior to this moment that they had been lied to. If a full autopsy had been performed, it would likely determine that the cause of death was poisoning by deadly nightshade. The individual who made these requests to be present was, of course, our own Layne Thompson. If this poisoning had, through CC TV or other observation—perhaps someone with an eidetic memory standing on a street corner noticing which direction he had come from—been traced back to the West End café where it had occurred and someone had gone through the bins out back, they would have found hand-torn leaves of belladonna, taken, I believe, from the Royal Botanic Gardens.'

Autumn made a low whistle of approval and received several disapproving stares.

'What?' Autumn asked, 'That sort of thing doesn't happen. It's impressive.'

'This happens to be the very same café where the playwright Ms. Shamira Allis is currently employed as a barista.'

Attention turned to Shamira. Richard wondered in that moment if he had ever really known her at all. Had she discovered that there was a production that could potentially ruin her if anyone worked out that some of the text was the same and set out to kill the director to make sure that it never made it to the stage?

'Based on the quantity of toxins extracted from the bin in the café—'

Kiran tried to hide a snicker. Ash ignored this.

'As opposed to the more typical period of a few days between ingesting organic poisons and death, the poisoning itself would have occurred less than four hours before the time of death. Ms. Allis does not work a shift on Saturdays.'

Richard let out an audible sigh of relief.

'This is where I give way to speculation. I believe, although, once again I do not have proof, that Douglas's poisoner posed as an employee of the coffee shop with the partial knowledge of the other employees. They were likely aware of this person's identity but not of their specific intentions that afternoon. Perhaps they claimed to be working a concept album about a barista. Kiran—'

Kiran let out a short gasp as though she had been punched. There was some muttering around the room, louder this time.

'What time did The Stone Dandelions soundcheck on the second?'

Kiran pulled a face thinking about how to answer the question. 'Um, well, we didn't really. They told us to get lost.'

'Who did?' Ash prodded.

'The stage crew,' Kiran said.

'Your own crew?' Ash wondered.

'Yes,' Kiran waved a hand. 'They didn't literally tell us to get lost, they just metaphorically told us to get lost.'

Ash frowned, 'Where would you have been between five and six in the afternoon?'

'Chipotle,' Kiran said simply.

Ash felt like their theories were threatening to fall apart in their hands. 'Chipotle? Which Chipotle?'

'Hang on, I've got a receipt,' Mila opened her bag and rummaged around for a couple of minutes until she located the crumpled and disintegrating receipt from weeks ago. She handed it to Ash.

Ash stared at the receipt and then, slowly, set it down beside the letter they had found in the hotel desk. 'Were all three of you at the Chipotle?'

'Those are each of our orders on there,' Mila said. 'I paid for it.'

Based on everything Ash had pieced together, the time on the receipt was about twenty minutes before when the poisoning was thought to have occurred. The address of the Chipotle was two and a half blocks away from the café.

'Were you all there the whole time until you had to go back to the theatre?' Ash asked.

Kiran thought about this. 'Didn't Layne go to the bathroom—toilet, whatever, at some point?' She thought some more. 'I'm not sure how long they were gone. Layne did you go multiple times? I don't remember. I think we got distracted talking about corporate monopolization.'

'I wasn't there the whole time,' Layne admitted—the first time they had spoken since everyone had gathered in the hotel room.

The pieces reshuffled for Ash and then fell into place. Ash met Layne's eyes. Layne nodded. Ash took a deep breath.

'After they had been at the Chipotle for some minutes, Layne Thompson told their bandmates they were going to the toilet, which they did, putting on a hat or wig so they would be less recognizable on the street. Then they exited the Chipotle, unnoticed by their bandmates who were engrossed in conversation, ran two blocks southwest, entered the café where Shamira Allis works and announced that they needed to start a shift in order to do 'research' and that they must not tell anyone else under any circumstances. The employees working that shift recognized Thompson and agreed with enthusiasm. Someone on the cast of *Roses and Thorns* had recommended the café to Robert Douglas on Layne's instruction. Layne served Mr. Douglas a salad containing lettuce, belladonna, Cesar's mushrooms, dressing and powdered belladonna and when he fled the café Layne briefly followed him out and then returned to the Chipotle where their friends were none the wiser.'

Kiran shook her head, amused. 'Layne did you really tell them you were doing "research"?'

Layne shrugged. 'It worked, didn't it?'

Ash turned to Morgan. 'Legal speaking does that constitute a murder confession?'

'No,' Morgan said. 'Legally that constitutes confessing that you told someone you were doing research.'

'Which is just as bad,' Mila said, because someone had to.

'There you have it,' Ash said, sitting down. 'Layne, would you like to keep the letter and the receipt?'

Layne stood up silently, picked up the documents and slipped them into their pocket.

A different sort of silence filled the room until Autumn asked, 'So, how are we all feeling about this?'

No one answered. Everyone looked at Layne.

'What do I have to do to get you to promise not to ever write any of this down?' Layne asked.

'Can I go onstage in Brighton?' Autumn requested. 'I've learned all the bass parts.'

'Is this an ultimatum?' Layne asked exhaustedly.

Autumn grinned, triumph within her grasp. 'Does it need to be?'

Richard raised his hand. Ash wondered how that had somehow become the convention—raising your hand when you had something to say. 'Er, yes, Richard?' Ash said.

'I would also like to make an ultimatum,' Richard announced. 'As we know, my girlfriend owes damages to the playwright Lilith Gibson. I'm asking Layne for money to pay those damages and legal fees.'

'Or else you'll have me arrested for murder?' Layne filled in the other half of the ultimatum.

Richard looked ashamed. 'I didn't want to say it.'

Layne raised an eyebrow. 'But you meant it. But you're threatening it.'

'Will you pay the fees and damages?'

'How much is it?' Layne was halfway to pulling out a chequebook.

'In total?'

Layne nodded. 'The whole sum.'

'A little over thirty thousand.'

'That's it? You could have just asked.'

Richard stared at them, too shaken to be frustrated. 'Layne, how much do you think you're paying me?'

'It's not much is it?'

'Not really, no.'

'You sure you don't want to throw a pay raise into the ultimatum?' Layne inquired.

Richard scratched his head. 'I think that would be unethical.'

'I'll pay your legal fees, but I mean it when I say you could have just asked.'

'I feel like I don't know you well enough to do that,' Richard said. He had only been working with Layne for a few weeks, eventful as those weeks might have been.

'I've got enough money to hire a personal publicist. I won't miss it.'

'I meant as an employer. I did not feel like I had a sense of how you would respond,' Richard said, still not sure how Layne would respond even to him saying this.

'Did you think I would fire you for asking?' Layne was genuinely puzzled.

'Many people would,' Richard pointed out.

'Just for asking?'

'It's a bit of an absurd thing to demand of your employer.'

'Fortunately, now you are in a position where you can present a murder case. How could I possibly refuse with a threat like that hanging over me?'

Richard wondered if he had made a mistake. It occurred to him that he could still go to the police with the knowledge of Robert's murder, no matter what concessions Layne made. Layne must be aware of this. Perhaps presenting this request in the form of an ultimatum would end up spoiling his working relationship with Layne Thompson. Was there any way their circumstances could go back to normal after this? He really did not like the knowledge that he was threating someone. How much trust could exist in a relationship where one person had the power to destroy another—but the more he thought about it, didn't everyone always possess the capacity to ruin other people's lives? Wasn't that what this was all about?

'I'm sorry,' Richard said.

'I accept your apology,' Layne smiled. 'I'm not that much of an out-of-touch millionaire.'

'I didn't think that you were,' Richard said, which was only true because he could not imagine fitting Layne into any preconceived stereotypes whatsoever.

'Only a little bit of an out-of-touch millionaire,' Layne amended because it was, to some extent, true.

'I'm very grateful.' Richard was wondering if he still had his job.

'I kind of wish you had asked for a pay raise too.'

'You can do that without my having to ask,' he pointed out.

'I know,' Layne agreed. 'I'll consider it.'

'I'm not really bothered either way as long as the lawsuit stuff is sorted out.'

'Are you sure?'

'Yes. You can do what you want as long as my girlfriend isn't in trouble anymore.'

'That's very valiant of you. Does anyone else have any ultimatums?'

There were some requests for more cups of tea and questions of when they would be allowed to go home.

'It's really alarming how much all of you trust me,' Layne said, feeling almost equally defeated as relieved.

'No,' Autumn said, 'what's really alarming is how much the cast of *Roses and Thorns* trusted you. The fact that you actually went through with would seem to be confirmation that whatever impression they had of you was accurate, which, really alarmingly, was something I had failed to pick up on. I had always considered you relatively stable, unhinged, perhaps, emotionally turbulent, but ultimately grounded and rational—'

'What makes you think this was not an ultimately grounded and rational action?' Layne demanded brightly.

'Everything you were saying to me about guilt and fear and how you felt about ruining a screenwriter's career because a handful of young people did not like his decision making and felt like their personal taste should be allowed to be the arbiter of who gets to make work,' Autumn explained.

'You did what to a screenwriter?' Morgan asked, intrigued. 'When was this?'

'Around nine years ago,' Layne said. 'In retrospect, I think some of the people I was listening to, some of the people I acted on the behalf of may have been overreacting.'

In the context, this was quite a worrying thing to hear. 'Do you think, perhaps, something similar happened this time, as well?' Autumn asked, half to be contentious, half out of actual concern.

A denser silence fell over the room.

'This time?' Layne asked, the question leaden in their mouth, plummeting through the silence once it was spoken aloud.

'You were acting on the behalf of others and taking their concerns as exactly as grievous as stated. In both cases, I believe you considered the stakes to be a matter of life and death—'

'It was a matter of life and death,' Layne said with a quiver of uncertainty.

'Well, it certainly was this time, after you got involved,' Autumn agreed.

Despite themself and maybe because of how worried they were, Morgan found themself laughing. Autumn grinned at them and then turned back to Layne, all seriousness.

'Is it possible that you made an error in judgment?' Autumn asked once again.

'Think of it this way,' Layne said, trying to salvage some semblance of a sense of certainty. 'How desperate do you have to be to go to a rockstar when you're looking for a hitman?'

'Desperate, or misguided?' Autumn asked.

'It's got to be both, doesn't it?' Layne said. 'I did what I did. I believe I did the right thing. You can try to convince me that I'm wrong, but I don't know how successful you would be and you're definitely going to need more evidence.'

'Is that also how you responded when you were questioned about how you responded to Sean Gorski's second feature film and spearheaded his denouncement?' Autumn asked.

'I fail to see how that reflects upon my present circumstances and recent actions,' Layne maintained.

'Some people think you're not very good at taking criticism,' Kiran added, before she could stop herself.

'They're right!' Layne agreed, almost shouting. 'I don't actually know how my ego got so damn fragile, but every so often I am reminded that it is and that I have to live with it. I feel horribly guilty about it, and I think that's just another extension of the same problem. Somehow who I am and what I'm capable of has become something so massive in my mind and instead of running away from it I'm afraid I've just toppled over the edge. I am constantly terrified that I'm getting everything wrong and then when someone says I have I just want to say that I am trying so hard, goddamn it, I am trying so goddamn hard, and that is exactly the wrong thing to say, and I know it but sometimes I say it anyway. I know that this is a problem. I wish I could take up less space in my own mind, but it doesn't work like that. That's not how accountability works. It's something I am working on and it really takes me by surprise sometimes. I think I've been told so many times that I lack an ego given, you know, everything, that I've started to believe it and then I end up being blindsided by my own pride and self-regard. It's a matter of simultaneously thinking that I'm not a particularly stuck up or self-endeared person but also knowing that when I get personally offended, I get cut to the quick. I don't know if it really is fragility or something else some different kind of faultline or insecurity. I don't think of myself as someone who spends my time worrying about what other people think of me. I think I'm independent and unimpressionable but I'm also someone who spends massive amounts of time worrying about what other people think. I'm not sure why all of this is happening. I haven't traced the causality. I don't know if it's some kind of chemical imbalance or a quick rise to prominence. I do know that I'm too good at simply agreeing when someone says I'm bad at taking criticism. I know that doesn't actually help anything.'

Everyone stared at Layne as though they had been expecting this outburst for a long, long time.

'I'm glad you know that,' Kiran said slowly.

'Part of the problem is that people respond like that because it makes me feel better,' Layne said.

'Is that actually the problem?' Autumn asked rhetorically.

'If I knew I would tell you,' Layne said, feeling like a cat had torn gaping holes in the burlap sack of their self-image that could never be sewn back together again no matter what kind of needle and thread you had brought to try to sort out the situation. 'My head hurts. Could you all please get out of my hotel room?'

Everyone stood up to go.

'If we go down to the bar I can buy a round of drinks,' Morgan offered.

'Count me in!' Autumn said and Layne had the feeling that these drinks were going to be thought of as celebratory rather than seeking respite. Well, that was alright, wasn't it? Everything was out on the table now. All the cards had been laid down.

'Actually, Ash?' Layne said, just before they were about to leave. 'Could I talk to you for a moment?'

'Alone in your hotel room?' Ash asked.

'Good point.' Layne looked around. 'Who would you like to stay?'

'Richard?' Ash suggested.

Richard sighed and sat back down in the swivel chair from the hotel desk. They picked up a bottle of prosecco from the minibar. 'I am going to drink this, though. I hope you don't mind.'

'Go ahead,' Layne said.

Richard popped the cork, dribbling foam onto the carpet.

'Ash, I'd like to thank you for how you handled that. You deserve better than getting wrapped up in the chaos that is my life.'

'I really don't mind. You are paying me for all of this after all.'

Richard raised the bottle. 'Cheers to getting paid.'

'I murdered someone. I understand if that has shattered your impression of me.'

'It's not so much shattered as confused,' Ash said. 'I think I haven't really processed it yet.'

'I completely understand if you want to cut all contact with me,' Layne said.

'Would you like me to? I can if you would want me to.'

'You're so reasonable about everything. I don't know how you do it.'

'If I behaved unreasonably, I would have to live with the impression of that moment forever. It teaches one patience pretty quickly.'

'Is that what it is?' Layne wondered.

'Honestly, I have no idea,' Ash admitted.

'Sometimes I wonder if I am the way that I am because I feel stuck,' Layne said, apparently finding out a new variation on the melodic theme of psychoanalyzing themselves.

Ash saw Richard roll his eyes behind Layne's back.

'Stuck? But you've made so much work. You're constantly doing something different,' Ash said.

Layne shook their head. 'Don't you understand? My work's not going anywhere. It's just running around in circles.'

'That's not true,' Ash breathed. 'Anyone who has heard anything you've worked on can see that's not true.'

'But it's not helping the world, is it?'

'It's helping so many people. I could start telling you what The Stone Dandelion's music has meant to me and it would take all week to get to the second subheading.'

'It's not effecting any actual material or policy change, is it?' Layne asked. 'It's not moving anything forward at all.'

'That's not the only way to do something to help the world. It's giving people something to hold onto. That's necessary. People need to feel like they have a way to express themselves, somewhere to go when pressures mount. Heck, even Morgan Garrett who has more belief in government than any of us has gone into acting.'

Layne frowned. 'Have they really?'

'Gone into acting? They're trying to,' Ash said.

'No, have they really got more belief in government than the rest of us?'

'They're a politician?' Ash felt a little confused. Who did Layne mean by 'the rest of us'? For that matter, who had Ash meant when they had said 'any of us'?

'Does that require belief in government?' Layne inquired seriously.

'It does if you're doing it the way the Morgan Garrett does.' This much was clear to Ash.

'Alright, fair enough. Do you think it counts as tax fraud if you donate to charities and then still pay your taxes?'

Ash shook their head. 'What does this have to do with anything?'

'I've been trying to think of things that I could do,' Layne explained uncertainly.

'Things that are not murder, you mean?'

Richard held up a glass they had found. 'Can I use this. You didn't put mouthwash in it or anything, did you?'

'Yes, things that are not murder,' Layne agreed.

'No murder in this glass,' Richard confirmed.

'You could always give money to people directly,' Ash pointed out. 'You know, I was wondering how I was going to end up bringing this up, but I actually have a favor that I would like to ask—I'm starting uni next year and I was wondering you would maybe want to visit the school a couple of times or do some kind of workshop or something like that. The students would really appreciate it I think.'

Richard spit a mouthful of prosecco back into the glass. 'Bleurgh. It tastes like washing up liquid. Disgusting.'

'Take it up with the hotel,' Layne suggested. 'It's not my washing up liquid. Not my mouthwash either.' They stood up and began to pace around the room frenetically, punctuating their thoughts with changes in direction, pivoting on the carpet. 'Music has a great deal of power, a massive amount of influence on people's emotional state and associations. It has to be used wisely. I often worry that I'm not in possession of that kind of wisdom. What if I'm just creating idle distractions that are getting in the way and wasting time and resources? The world is in a bad way— It's on course to get even— No, that's disingenuous, that's bad theory and hopelessness is not something that we have time to indulge in— Or do we? Is it alright to take the time to grieve? That can't be wrong, can it to acknowledge what we have lost, what we're not going to be able to save. We've got to make space for that emotion too, right, because it's something people are experiencing. We just can't allow ourselves to get bogged down in inertia.'

'I agree with that!' Ash said wholeheartedly. 'I don't even think hope is necessary for trying anyway. Trying is imperative, though, trying is necessary. To keep going is the important thing, to keep striving, to never give in to thinking that making change doesn't matter, that it's not worth it. Anyone's life you make better is worth it. There is a right and wrong side of history, and the lines aren't where most people think they are. You and I know that. We know that intimately.'

'Thank you for saying that, Ash, it means a lot.'

Richard had gone back to drinking out of the prosecco bottle, having given up on the glass as a lost cause.

Ash nodded. 'And what you do is original and unique, too. You have a perspective that no one else does but a lot of people can relate to it very, very deeply. Sometimes I think more deeply than you even intend. I'll always be fucking weirdo; you'll always be a fucking weirdo and that's part of why what we do matters. Not in any kind of self-important way, we just have something new to bring to the table and that's worthwhile in itself.'

'You sound so wise,' Layne sighed. 'How did you get to sound so wise?'

Ash smirked shyly. 'I remember every soundbite of wisdom I have ever heard, remember?'

'Is that what it is?' Layne smiled.

'I told you I didn't know but there's more where it came from. Not everything has to be revolutionary to be worth doing, but that is no reason, that is never a reason to shy away from doing something that could actually shift the goalposts. Convention is never any reason to run from what your heart is telling you to do. The fact that you can just about barely fit into the box that they've made for you is not a reason to stay there. Danger and fear are reasons to stay, reasons not to move. Danger is real. Fear is real too, it is a physiological fact. You should be aware of what danger you are actually putting yourself in. You should be very clear-sighted about that. Life is so often at stake. I think we know how often life is at stake. That's part of why people need something to hold onto. Because we remember everyone who hasn't made it and we want to be able help whoever might need someone in the future. We want to do right by our present and future selves as well.'

'I know I've got people who count on me,' Layne said, biting their lip worriedly, 'And I cannot let them down. I'm terrified of even disappointing them in anyway or letting them down and letting them think that I'm not that I'm not the person that they hoped I was. Again, I don't think this is about me, I think it's about their hopes and dreams and not shattering them. That's part of why I did everything that I did. I wanted to figure out what I could to do get out of everyone around me seeming me as some kind of idealized version of myself that they've made up in their head. Only I wanted to do it without anyone feeling betrayed.'

A moment of silence stretched across the hotel room. It was snapped by Ash asking, 'So, you went with murder?'

'I didn't think anyone was sitting around thinking "I know Layne Thompson isn't a murderer!" Because it's not the sort of thing that most people do but it might just be something they could see me doing.'

'Why—' Ash stopped to reconsider this question. 'I mean, I'm not saying you're wrong, you have written a lot of murder-y songs.'

'I have?' Layne tried to tally up on their fingers how many lyrics they had written involving murder. They ran out of fingers.

'It's one of the main bones anyone has to pick with you,' Ash said with the certainty of someone who could recite the exact complaints and criticisms they were thinking of.

'Is that so?'

'I've read all the forums.'

'I guess you're right. Do people still read forums?'

'It's mainly Reddit,' Ash considered.

'That makes sense.'

Ash shook their head in disbelief. 'It's like you've tried to put up so high a wall between fact and fiction that you've ended up toppling over the edge and landing so much harder than you expected.'

'I still think I was right in the end,' Layne said resolutely.

'I'm not saying you did the wrong thing; I'm just saying that you killed someone.'

'I know I killed someone.' Layne was matter of fact.

Lounging in the swivel chair, Richard inspected how much sparkling wine was left in the bottle.

'Who were you going to try to pin it on?' Ash asked.

'I wasn't trying to pin it on anyone. I was hoping that it would be written off as unsuspicious and then it was. I was entirely successful. No one suspected anything at all, and I felt the guilt consuming me from the inside.'

'I thought you said you were rock-solid that you had done the right thing,' Ash pointed out.

'I was terrified someone would actually find out what had happened and that someone else would be sentenced.'

'Did you know how long it would take me to figure it out?' Ash asked.

'I didn't know that you would figure it out, I just suspected that probably would. You seemed my most likely chance.'

'Your most likely chance to be found out as a murderer? Are you sure there isn't some overhanging guilt about something else that is driving this whole thing?' Ash was vaguely aware of how absurd this sounded even as they said it. 'Something you did years ago that has been eating away at you all this time?'

'I've been trying to explain this the whole time. It was never just one thing. It was a hundred little things. It was never an attitude or a point of view that I regretted holding, it was an accumulation of uncertainty that I found, for the first time that I couldn't channel into anything productive.' Layne realised they were only putting this together just now.

'So, you poisoned someone?'

Layne massaged their temples. 'The murder was productive. This isn't about the murder. It's about everything else.'

'Are you sure? What changed? What made you feel like you were not getting anywhere anymore?' Ash was trying to find out what they could do to help.

'This is what I have been trying to tell you,' Layne said, not sure what it was they had been trying to communicate. 'You're just not believing me.'

'I believe you. I just don't understand it yet. I think. I'm not even quite sure that I actually know what you're talking about,' Ash said, which confirmed to Layne that they were on the same page after all.

'I think I'm talking about what I believe. What do you believe?'

Ash considered this, and then said carefully, 'I don't believe irony is a poison. I believe you can walk into the dark and take comfort in it. I believe loving and hating someone are often two sides of the same passion. I think there's a lot that can be accomplished with your tongue firmly in your cheek. Taking things seriously is not mutually exclusive with taking the mickey.'

Layne nodded. 'Those are good things to believe. Sometimes I just want to get paid to make music.'

'You disappoint me,' Ash said, not even quite sure why they said it.

'Because I murdered someone?'

'No, I can understand murder, but I can't let it go if you've succumbed to becoming a sellout.' Ash forced the words out through gritted teeth, before breaking out into a broad grin.

'You can understand murder?' Richard wondered, swirling the last of the prosecco.

'That's not the point,' Ash stressed.

'You see! I knew that they wouldn't care if you had done it!' Richard cried. 'Mind you, they're accusing you of selling out,' Richard gestured with the nearly empty bottle.

'That's not worse than murder,' Layne said.

'Isn't it?' Richard asked.

'You can't swing a dead cat in this business without getting accused of selling out,' Layne scoffed.

'Maybe you shouldn't swing dead cats,' Richard said reasonably.

Downstairs in the bar, Morgan and Autumn were hitting it off. Morgan had bought a round of elaborate cocktails that Shamira had not realised they sold at hotel bars.

'I just think it's fascinating being in proximity to such unusual minds.' Autumn said conspiratorially. 'I feel like Layne must have been the only person who would ever have responded to the letter those actors sent.'

'And they knew it! They made a judgment call and they were right! Isn't that extraordinary?' Morgan marveled.

'Do you like podcasts?' Autumn asked.

'Oh, I love podcasts,' Morgan said.

'What about true crime?'

'True crime writing? Reporting?'

'Podcasts,' Autumn specified.

'That might be something I could look into,' Morgan considered.

'I've got one.'

'A crime?'

'A podcast.'

'A true crime podcast?' Morgan asked, beaming.

'It's very well received. Majority five star audience reviews.'

'What do you focus on?'

'Strange cases. Ones where there's something unusual. *Outré*, even. Sometimes this means magicians completing rituals with sacrificial blood. Other times it means bodies found without their faces or locked rooms inside of other locked rooms.'

'So, murders then?' Morgan asked.

'Not just murders. I'm interested in all sorts as long as it isn't commonplace. As long as it isn't predictable and there's something mysterious about it.' Autumn lowered her voice which she thought made her sound mysterious and alluring.

'So, how did it compare?' Morgan wondered.

'How did what compare?'

'What Layne did. The events of the past couple of weeks—even the plagiarism case if you want to think of that as part of it—how did it compare to your standards?'

Autumn was delighted by this question. 'Would you like me to assign it a grade? Points out of ten?'

'It fell short, didn't it?' Morgan guessed.

'I thought it might be getting somewhere more interesting and then I felt like it kept taking wrong turns and ended up having far too much hanging on coincidence.'

'There was an extraordinary amount of coincidence, wasn't there? Perhaps that is interesting in itself?' Morgan offered.

Autumn shook her head. 'Coincidence doesn't make things more interesting; it makes them less interesting because it means there isn't actually anything connecting the points together, they just happen to be close to each other.'

Morgan made a sound of understanding. 'I can see what you mean by that. The story ends up being simpler rather than more complicated.'

'Do you also like it when things get complicated?' Autumn said, leaning forward passionately.

'I love it,' Morgan said.

Shamira set down her glass on the bar, loudly, uncomfortably, spilling some of her drink over the rim. Autumn and Morgan seemed to have forgotten that she was there. 'Would you two like me to go?' she asked.

'If you'd like to,' Autumn said airily.

'You're welcome to stay if you want,' Morgan said, trying to be polite.

Shamira stood up. 'I'm going to go see if they're done upstairs,' she said.

'Well, that's the wonderful thing about life, isn't it?' Autumn observed.

'What is?' Morgan asked breathily.

'You can always make it more complicated,' Autumn said softly.

Morgan raised their glass in a toast. 'To the complications!'

Autumn raised her own glass. 'And to being able to see them through the watch face.'

'They wouldn't really be complications if you couldn't see them, though, would they?' Morgan wondered. 'They have to be serving additional functions to be watch complications.'

'But what if they're…unwatched complications?' Autumn suggested. No one groaned. If anything, Morgan grinned even more broadly.

'I'm not sure that counts as a pun on the grounds that it doesn't make any sense. But you're not really disappointed though, are you?' Morgan smirked.

'No, I'm not,' Autumn agreed.

***

Upstairs, Shamira knocked on the door of the hotel room and Richard answered it, noticeably drunk.

'Wouldn't it be wonderful if all problems could be sorted out this neatly?' Richard asked in a dynamic state of bittersweet maudlin joy.

'No,' Shamira said. 'It wouldn't. Let's go home.'

'Layne killed a cat,' Richard hiccupped.

'No, I didn't.'

'Just a man,' Ash said coolly, unconsciously echoing Richard's drunken tones. 'I'm glad that she did. I believe he deserved it.'

'You should head home too,' Shamira told Ash.

'Just think, if she hadn't killed him, we would have a totally different point of view on so many things right now,' Ash offered.

This puzzled Shamira. 'Would we?' she asked.

'Richard wouldn't be drunk, for one thing, and Layne, and I would not know what Richard was like when he was drunk.'

'I suppose that is true,' Shamira conceded. 'But I fail to derive a larger moral from it.'

'But think about it, if I were to ask you if you thought that murder was wrong, and you did not know what Layne had done, you would give a different answer wouldn't you?'

'No.' Shamira shook her head. 'I would give exactly the same answer. I tend to think about things before I form opinions.'

'She's very admirable like that,' Richard said, snuggling up against Shamira.

'Thank you, dear.'

'Well,' Layne said. 'I feel like I'm in a different place even if no one else does.'

'Oh, I didn't say that,' Shamira said. 'I think we're all in quite a different place. This hotel for one thing.'

'I feel like I don't really understand you which is not at all how I felt a couple of days ago,' Ash said. 'I thought we would understand each other, and we have, but not at all in the way I thought I would.'

'That's very interesting.' Layne said. 'I feel like I've just pried myself open and I have no idea how to put myself back together.'

'Let's see how you feel after the show in Brighton,' Shamira said. 'With Autumn on bass.'

'Oh God,' Layne said, the implications hitting home. 'They're part of the touring band now, aren't they?'

'And it looks like Morgan might be tagging along, if you know what I mean?'

'Tremendous,' Layne said, shaking their head. 'I'm going to bed. Wake me when it's time to go.'

'I'm not your PA, I'm your PR,' Richard objected.

'See you in the morning,' Layne said.

They closed the door, and, in some inexplicable way, it did feel like nothing would ever be the same again. They were all in it together now. They knew what went on beneath the surface, and they could never hide in quite the same way that they always had before.

Acknowledgements

My first debt is to my first reader and line-editor, Oakley Swinson, for her eagle-eyed notes.

I learned how to be the writer I am with and from my fellow playwrights at the National Theater Institute: Daryn, Grace, Holly, Ish, Katsuto and Kota.

I would like to thank the cast of the film adaptation of this novel: Ana, Atrix, Bre, Danica, Daryn, Elise, Jennifer, Kait, Kota, Levi, Oakley and Tess for inspiring and sticking with me.

I'd also like to thank those who witnessed and provided a sounding board for the genesis of this project at Rose Bruford College: Sophia, Teresa, Austin, Jacob, Jenette, Jennifer, Lisa, Lucia, Ryan, and Dorothy for providing perspective and intrigue.

Many thanks to my parents for supporting me and watching and reading so many cozy mysteries and detective stories — like, hundreds of them.

Made in the USA
Monee, IL
14 July 2023

39293648R00089